SHADOWS OF THE PAST

Women Of Strength Series (Book 2)

Lucy Appadoo

This book is dedicated to the victims of family secrets and stalking.

May they get justice for their suffering.

It is also dedicated to my supportive husband and two daughters.

Contents

Chapter 1

DISTURBING NEWS

Daniela stretched out in bed, yawning as the sun filtered in through her bedroom. Summer had begun in Spain, and she savoured the early light. She rose from bed, put on a dressing gown and rubbed her eyes. Still tired, she regretted staying up late last night, talking with Blanca about her business expansion plans. Her phone by the bedside displayed six o'clock as she went to the kitchen and put bread in the toaster. Once it popped up, she spread jam on it, then pulled out a cup and poured espresso coffee with low-fat milk. While sipping on her steaming coffee, her friend and housemate, Blanca, came in.

"Hey, how did you sleep?" Blanca walked zombie-like into the kitchen, yawning. She dropped a slice of bread into the toaster.

"Okay, I guess." Daniela answered, scanning her roommate. "I haven't seen Carlos in a while. How are things between you guys?"

Blanca buttered her toast and sat across from her. She held the cup with both hands and blew on her coffee. "He's been busy with his photography business, but we've been great. I love him more every day. Who would have thought he'd move here?"

Daniela leaned forward. "I am amazed at how you two met in Brazil and now you're both back here. That's true love."

She smiled. "It is, and you will find yours soon."

Daniela shook her head. "I love your idealism, girl. But no. The man who will stay loyal to me is not out there"

Blanca finished her coffee. "Not all men are like your father, Daniela."

She winced. Why ruin her morning, thinking about a man who stopped caring for his wife and two daughters? She had moved on with her life.

Daniela's phone rang. "Hey, Mum. What's up?" Silence. "Mum? Are you there?"

Sobs filled the line. "Dani. Can you come over please?"

Her chest tightened. Something wasn't right. "Is Eva okay?"

"Eva's fine, darling. But please. Come over. The police need to speak to you, and I don't want to tell you over the phone. Just get here." *The police!* Before she could reply, her mother ended the call.

Daniela felt a heaviness deep in the pit of her stomach. "I have to go, Blanca. Would you mind ringing Sofia and getting her to take over at the dance studio for me today?"

Blanca nodded. "Of course. What happened?"

Daniela put her dishes in the sink. "I don't know, but my mum's upset about something. She wouldn't tell me over the phone. Probably because she thinks I'll have an accident if I hear bad news. Anyway, I'll talk to you later." Rushing to her room, she quickly dressed, then jumped into her sporty car and drove as fast as she could.

She reached her mother and sister's home in Puente De Vallecas in fifteen minutes. She wondered why a police car was parked at the curb. The warm wind brushed her flushed cheeks as she walked up the cracked concrete path. Waiting on the doorstep, she felt as if she was being watched. She shrugged it off, and after what felt like an hour, her mother answered the door.

Her mother, Adriana, ran a hand through her wavy, shoulder-length hair; black tinged with grey. Wispy strands had fallen to the sides of her face and her eyes were blood-shot.

Adriana wrapped her in her arms, holding her tight. "Mother, what is it?" She pulled away and followed her mother to the kitchen where two police officers sat at the table, holding cups of coffee.

They rose, looking glum. One officer was short and mousy-looking, while the other was average height with freckles and a moustache.

The short officer said, "I'm Officer Rodriguez."

"And I'm Officer Fernandez." He looked briefly at his partner. "We are very sorry to inform you that your father died late last night."

Daniela's legs wobbled as if she'd fall any minute. Fernandez held her arms and led her to the chair. Her vision blurred and nausea overcame her. Surely, she hadn't heard right. "What did you say?"

Fernandez's expression softened. "Your father appeared to have died in his sleep from unknown causes. We are very sorry for your loss."

Daniela turned to her mother who poured out fresh tears. "Was he sick? He couldn't have just died from unknown causes. Will there be an autopsy?"

Rodriguez nodded. "Yes, there will be an autopsy due to the sudden nature of his death. We can keep you abreast of the results. But for now, we have to ask you a few questions."

Daniela's body turned numb. She didn't know how to feel, as she had after her father had left them. Her mother joined her at the table and held her hand. The officers sat down again, making the kitchen appear even more cramped than usual. "We haven't seen my father for six years, so I don't know what to tell you."

Rodriguez nodded. "We need to rule out foul play. We'd like your perspective about your father's departure from your home. Do you know why he left? We asked your mother, but we need your perspective. You might have understood something else entirely."

Daniela briefly closed her eyes, thinking back to the night before he left. "He said goodnight to me in bed the night before and kissed me many times. I didn't understand then why he was so affectionate, but I understand it now. He was saying goodbye, but he was too gutless to tell me to my face."

"I see," said Rodriguez. "Has he been in touch with you recently?"

Daniela knit her brows. "No, I haven't heard from him. I had no idea of his whereabouts, Officer. What he did in the last three years is a mystery."

Her mother leaned forward. "Are all these questions really necessary? My daughter and I would like to grieve in private."

Fernandez intervened. "It is protocol that we question all family members, and to rule you both out as suspects. We will need to return to question your other daughter. Do you know what time she'll be returning from her work trip? You mentioned that she will be back tonight?"

"Yes, Officer," said her mother. "At around nine o'clock, but she won't have anything new to tell you."

Fernandez nodded. "We are still bound by law to return and question all family members. We also found something of interest in his home." He sipped the last of his coffee, then put the cup down. "A crossword puzzle by his side in bed. It had been completed, and Daniela's name was written on it. Did he like crossword puzzles?"

Her mother nodded. "He enjoyed crosswords, and used to do them with Daniela sometimes. It was their bonding time." She whimpered and bowed her head.

Daniela sighed. "It might have been an old puzzle we did together."

The officers stood. "We'll be in touch with the autopsy results," said Rodriguez. "Once we can release the body, you can make funeral arrangements."

Daniela closed the door behind them, threw herself into her mother's arms and cried her heart out.

Chapter 2

NEWS STORY

Rafael carried the worst hangover of his life into the office of *Le Vardadera Noticia* newspaper. He had spent the evening before watching football on TV and drinking scotch after scotch with his friend and boss. He took a few deep breaths, and rubbed his temples to soothe the stabbing pain and throb in the back of his head as he sat at his desk. At least he was the first in the office that morning and could enjoy the quiet. Soon, the long grey desks would fill with the other reporters and editors, and a hubbub of activity and noise.

Curtains drawn across the windows blocked out the morning light, except for those at the far end of the room, which gave a view of the Madrid city centre. Thankfully, the carpet muffled the footsteps as staff members dribbled into the newsroom. Someone flicked on the lights hanging from the ceiling and brightened the room.

Rafael needed strong coffee. Legs unsteady, he walked to the staff room, put a mug in the machine and clicked the button for an espresso. He closed his eyes to savour the bitter liquid that warmed his stomach. With a shaky hand, he returned to his desk to check his emails.

While deleting spam, the subject line of one email seized his attention: *embezzlement*. When he opened it, he saw that the message was a one-liner: *Not who he appeared to be*. It came with an attachment, a spreadsheet file. Who'd be sending him emails about this type of subject? Or it might be a prank. He got a lot of those in his spam messages.

He ran the malware-checking program, and when it was done and opened the verified file, Rafael saw financial statements. Every week for three years, someone named Abel Lopez had deposited two hundred Euros into a cash account. It amounted to a lot of money. Small amounts so as not to be noticed, but it was clear that the money was coming from a financial analyst company he recognized. *Finanzas de Armonia*. He didn't know who Abel Lopez was, but he resolved to find out.

Footsteps interrupted his thoughts. "Hi Rafael. You're in earlier than usual," Blanca said as she walked in, looking pale. He enjoyed working with Blanca. She was an amazing journalist with strong ethics and a can-do attitude. She worked on human interest stories, and the hectic pace of a daily newspaper meant he never knew what she was writing about until the article appeared in print. "Do you ever sleep?"

Rafael decided to keep the mysterious email to himself until he figured out what it was about. "Of course, I do," he answered, closing the file as she approached his desk. "I get at least four hours a night. Plenty for me to get enough energy for the next day. What about you? Getting little sleep, too, I'd say by the looks of those dark circles under your eyes. Is Carlos keeping you up at night?"

Blanca chuckled. "Seriously? My private life with Carlos is none of your concern," she said jokingly. "What are you looking at?"

He shrugged. "Nothing." He picked up research notes from his in-tray. "I have to finish the article about that burglary. Not to mention a hundred other things I need to do; ringing sources, verifying facts, that sort of stuff."

Blanca nodded. "I hear you, but take a break, too. I'm sure Fernando will understand that you have a life." She headed to the staff room.

Rafael returned to his computer, searching for the finance company he had read about in one of the earlier editions of the newspaper. He found the firm, *Finanzas de Armonia*. Clicking *Services* on the top menu, he scanned the names of the staff, but he didn't find Abel Lopez. This had to be the company, but the man must no longer work for them. Slouching, he did an internet search for Abel Lopez, but all he found were news stories about awards and accolades he'd received for his work as a financial analyst and saving companies who were on the brink of bankruptcy. That was ironic if he embezzled as the email claimed.

His phone buzzed, the display showing his boss and drinking buddy, Fernando. "Hey, man. What's up? It's only seven-thirty."

"I'm texting you an address. We have a story. Can't explain now. Get to it."

"On it, boss." He ended the call and headed to the underground car park. He still couldn't decide whether the email was a lead, or fake news. He got false leads all the time and he didn't plan on wasting his time on trolls.

As he drove his black Audi to the address in Fernando's text, he wondered whether his friend ever slept. This wasn't the first time he'd called this early in the morning for a story. But he appreciated the early calls from Fernando as they usually meant an important assignment, and he'd want Rafael to get into the story before the rival newspapers.

As a journalist, Rafael thrived on investigating controversial topics, and used his contacts in the police department as well as other sources to verify statements. He had developed a reputation as the reporter who got stories fast enough for the next day's newspaper. His beat was general news, and he wanted to be known for his balanced stories. He had won an award for a story about a political protest.

Rafael preferred to delve deeper into crime stories, but sometimes wondered whether it was heartless of him to hope for people's suffering so he could get that bigger and better story.

At his destination in the centre of Madrid, Rafael saw police officers outside a villa-like, two-storey house, talking to an older woman who wiped her eyes and shook her head. Neighbours on either side watched.

He made a beeline for the young neighbour on the right side of the house. She had blue eyes and wore a dressing gown. She had to have heard something.

"Hello, Miss. I'm Rafael, a reporter from *Le Vardadera Noticia*. Do you know what happened here?"

She nodded. "I overheard the housekeeper saying that Abel was dead."

Rafael's blood turned cold and he ignored the tightness in his chest. "I'm sorry, did you say Abel? What was his surname, and did you know the man?"

She tightened the belt on her robe and looked at the house. "I did know him, and the surname is Lopez. Abel Lopez." She sighed and placed a hand over her chin. "He was a nice man who kept to himself. He was always busy with his work but always said hello when we saw each other outside. It's such a shock." She focused on the front entrance of her house as a little boy wandered outside. "Listen, I wish I could tell you more. But I need to go."

He nodded. "Thank you for your time." Rafael waited until the older woman he assumed was the housekeeper stepped away from the officers. "Excuse me, miss." He introduced himself. "Can you tell me what happened here?"

The lady's hands shook and her high ponytail fell down in a tangled mess as she threaded her hands through the back of it. She appeared to be in her sixties. "Abel was a good man, and did not deserve this. Not at all. I clean his house twice a week." Tears streamed down her cheeks. "This morning, I arrived to find him dead in his bed. The police don't know what happened, but they will investigate. Oh, dear Lord! He was such a nice man and so young, too. How could he die like this? Such a shame. On his own. No family by his side."

"Do you know how it happened?"

She shook her head roughly. "No, I don't know. The police will investigate. Sorry, but I have to go."

He handed her a business card. "If you remember anything else, please call me."

The lady nodded. "Such a shame really. Too young to die." She rushed off and got into a compact car, sniffling all the way.

He had the makings of a big story here if this death wasn't accidental or natural, but who had sent him that email about the victim?

Chapter 3

FRIENDSHIP

Daniela sat with her hands clasped in her lap, watching people enter the restaurant. Sunlight streamed through the wide bay windows, illuminating paintings of famous artists and celebrities on the walls. Rough-timber tables came with matching chairs. She took a deep breath on seeing a towering man whose eyes briefly bore into hers. Wearing a well-pressed suit, he strutted to the counter. The man reminded her of her father. She didn't need to dwell on such reminders and shook those thoughts away to concentrate on the menu.

It had been a week since the police had told her about her father's death under suspicious circumstances, but she still awaited the autopsy results. She had to keep living her life and not think about a man who had abandoned them six years ago. Leaving without a word. Without a note. Without an explanation.

Over the years, she had racked her brain to figure out what had caused him to leave, but she couldn't think of anything. It had been unlike him to leave like that, especially after he'd quit drinking alcohol. He'd changed.

She pressed a finger to her temple to soothe the tension in her head as Blanca and another friend, Kim, headed towards her. She rose to hug them both.

"I want to say again, Daniela, how sorry I am about your father," Kim said. "Are you okay?" Kim sat across the table, her dark brown eyes and full, pouting lips displaying a sweet and innocent attractiveness. Her family was Chinese and had arrived in Madrid when she was a young child. Jet black hair draped neatly down her shoulders.

Blanca's green eyes burned into Daniela's. "I wish I could do more for you."

Daniela gave her a reassuring smile, a warmth penetrating her chest. She didn't know what she'd do without her friends. They had both endured their own traumas. "I am meeting with my sister and mum later tonight, having a few friends and family over to give their condolences." She rubbed her hands together and fought the sharp pain in her back. "I still can't believe it. After all these years, he dares to come back into our lives only to crush us again.

Kim leaned forward, her dainty fingers resting underneath her chin. "The autopsy results will give you answers."

Blanca squared her shoulders. "I am sorry about that article by my colleague, Rafael. If I had known what he was writing, I would have put a stop to it. But the information checks out, Daniela."

A slim waitress approached. Blanca ordered hot chocolate, and the others ordered coffee and sweets to share.

Daniela turned to Blanca. "It's not your fault, but the jerk could have waited until we had a bit of time to grieve. It was out there straight off the bat, him embezzling money and getting away with it for all these years. I hate not only my father, but that damn reporter, too. I hate him with a passion." Bile rose in her throat. "If I never meet that jerk you work with, it'll be too soon." She didn't want to be associated with a man who supposedly embezzled money. Shame overwhelmed her as she thought about her father possibly committing a crime. She clenched her fists and briefly closed her eyes to shut off the burning pain in her chest.

Kim shook her head. "This will die down, Daniela. Give it time." She caressed her friend's hand, offering a reassuring smile.

She bowed, staring into her hands. "What I don't get is that my father put money into our accounts a couple of years back, with strict instructions to a lawyer that it not be returned. We didn't know how to find him anyway. I deposited the money into an investment account, and it's earned some interest. I felt guilty about the money, but then I thought, hell, he abandoned us for no reason. Why shouldn't he have contributed and helped us succeed in life?" She shook her head. "I don't understand why he would embezzle money when he made a good living in his profession."

Blanca nodded. "I hear you, Dani, but I am sure you'll eventually get answers."

Daniela tried to make sense of that article, ignoring the chills in her spine. "You mentioned your colleague had a source, but how reliable is it?"

"It was backed up by your father's employer, who did their own investigating, not to mention the proof in the paperwork. I am sorry."

Daniela frowned, her eyes darkening. She was about to speak up when the waitress brought over their hot drinks and churros. When she had walked away, Daniela leaned forward. "I just have to put it out of my mind. Clear my head and think about other things. Tonight, I'll be there for my family. Then when we have the funeral, we'll give him a proper send-off. In spite of what he did, he was still my father."

Blanca nodded. "As Kim said, give yourself the time to grieve, and know that we're here for you." Her eyes focused on Kim for a moment as if they were hiding a secret.

Daniela stared. "What's going on?"

Blanca glanced nervously at her before refocusing on Kim. "I spoke to Rafael, and he wants to apologise for writing that article so soon."

Daniela ignored the tightness in her chest and quivering hands. "I don't need an apology. What's done is done, and I just need to move on."

Blanca's eyes turned a shade darker. "He insists on meeting you to apologise."

Daniela sipped her drink, thinking about the other articles this reporter had written. He was a gifted writer, but that didn't mean she had to like him for aggravating their grief. "Fine. I'll give him a damn piece of my mind, then hopefully he'll stay out of my way and not write anything else about my father."

Blanca smiled. "I will set a time for him to come over. Thanks, Daniela. He's not a bad guy. A bit ambitious, but he's been nice to me since I've known him."

Kim shifted. "Listen, why don't you start back at my yoga studio? I have the perfect class for you next week. You need to destress. What do you think?"

Daniela smiled. "Maybe. We'll see." She needed the distraction. But she wasn't looking forward to meeting this reporter, Rafael. He sounded t too ambitious and cut-throat for her liking.

Chapter 4

GRIEF

Daniela opened the front door nervously to see a tall man with jet-black hair in a crew cut that brought out his dark, piercing brown eyes. His large hands held a manila folder, and the way his tight black jeans and white, fitted shirt pressed against his well-toned muscles made her stomach tingle. His awkward smile brought out the dimples in his cheeks.

What was she doing? This guy was the enemy, and she was checking him out like he was a piece of meat to be eaten.

Where was Blanca? She had organised this meeting. Daniela needed support and refused to talk to this arrogant man on her own. Taking a deep breath, she was about to shut the door when Blanca came out from within the house, giving her a reassuring smile.

Blanca pushed forward and hugged the tall man. "Rafael. Good to see you. Come in." She brought him to their sofa and sat beside him while Daniela sat on the armchair opposite. "This is my dear friend, Daniela." She faced her colleague. "This is Rafael Martin."

Rafael rose slightly and put out his hand. "Pleased to meet you, Daniela. I am sorry for your loss" She turned away and ignored it. His eyes bore into her own.

"Just say your damn piece and then leave," Daniela said.

Blanca cleared her throat. "Why don't I make us a cup of coffee." She went to the kitchen, leaving them alone.

Daniela's body shook as if she was cold, but the air in the room was warm. "Kindly explain to me why you'd tarnish a dead man's name when his family is grieving?"

Rafael pressed his hands into his legs, glancing after Blanca as if she could rescue him. "I apologise, but I was just doing my job. It's the name of the game, and I had facts to back it up. It was not a baseless article, but a factual one." He shifted. "It's my job and I do it well." He played with the collar of his shirt and avoided her eyes.

Daniela couldn't believe the arrogance that seemed to ooze from him. *He does it well?* "You know, it could have waited until we'd processed the news. My father had his faults, but he was a good man. And I wonder if you do have your facts straight."

He angled his head. "So good that he left his family. Interesting perspective."

Daniela pushed down her rage, clenching her hands and gritting her teeth. She had to compose herself or she didn't know what she'd say. What was taking Blanca so long? "You do not know anything about my father. Not a clue, Mr. Martin."

He pressed his lips together and narrowed his eyes. Rubbing the back of his neck, he fixed his eyes hard on Daniela. "I know how to do my job, Ms. Lopez, and that is reporting the facts. I don't need you telling me what I should and shouldn't write."

Blanca returned with a tray and set it on the table. She handed both Rafael and Daniela cups of coffee. The doorbell rang and she rushed to the door. "That'll be Carlos."

Carlos walked in, pressed his body against Blanca's and kissed her long and hard. He pulled away from her and flicked his dark hair out of his eyes. "Hi, Daniela." She smiled at him and he kissed her on the cheek. He was a man with principles, and his love for Blanca shone through. Then he slapped Rafael on the shoulder. "It's good to see you, man."

Rafael stood up and shook Carlos's hand. "Hey, Carlos. How's the photography business going?" Daniela wasn't surprised that they knew each other, as Carlos visited Blanca at the newspaper often.

"It's doing well. Luiz is keeping it going in Brazil. We make it work." He cleared his throat. "We might consider expanding the business soon into other countries. You can join us if you like." He sat next to Blanca and brought her hand to his lips. She blushed.

Oh, young love. Daniela remembered how she thought she had loved her ex-boyfriend, Esteban. But he had proved to be like her father. Abandoned her without a reason, other than saying he needed to find himself and wasn't ready to commit. He had broken her heart, but she recovered well, resolving that she would no longer let herself be pulled into love without following her intuition.

Rafael laughed. "I have a marketing background, Carlos, but those days are long behind me. I love investigative reporting."

"Speaking of marketing ..." Blanca turned to Daniela. "My friend here is planning to expand her business. She has a dance school that's doing well. You might be able to give her some pointers on how to promote it better."

Daniela glared at her friend. How could she do such a thing? "I do not need help. Especially from a man who doesn't have any principles."

Rafael's face tightened and he crossed his arms. "I have principles, but I write about the facts. Emotions do not play a part in good reporting. I believe you should know that."

Daniela scoffed. "But how about providing a balanced perspective regarding a man who had a family and worked hard in his job? Why not report on that?" She didn't let him respond. "Oh, I know. Because that wouldn't sell newspapers, would it?"

Carlos looked at Blanca with a raised eyebrow. "Daniela, I know I have said this before, but I am so sorry for your loss. Emotions are running high now. We need to take a breather here."

Blanca frowned. "I am sorry, guys. I shouldn't have done this so soon. Daniela, you're still grieving, and I rushed this meeting." She gave Rafael a reassuring smile. "Maybe we can do this another time, Rafael. I'm sorry, but Daniela needs time."

Daniela got up and put her hands on her hips, fighting back tears. "I do not need time, Blanca. I know a self-absorbed, egotistical man when I see one. He's just like—" Why was she about to mention Esteban? It was none of this creep's business. If she never saw him again, it would be too soon. "Sorry, Blanca, Carlos, but I can't do this." She scurried out of the living room, down the corridor and into her room, and slammed the door behind her. Throwing herself on the bed, she let the tears fall.

Chapter 5

NEW ARTICLE

R afael tapped out an outline for a new article a few days later. The clicking of his computer keyboard mingled with the voices of other reporters, some on the phone, while others chatted to co-workers about new stories. He could also hear the digital subscription team having a meeting in a nearby conference room.

He'd spent the day after meeting with Daniela fuming and wondering how she could be that angry with him. More was going on with her, and he'd been in the firing line. How dare she say those things to him when she didn't even know him? Assuming he was arrogant and had no principles. He had principles, but he also had a job to do, and he planned to do bigger and better things in his career. Another award or two wouldn't go astray. Daniela would not foil his ambitions just because she was grieving and couldn't see straight. He had a story and went with it. It was his job and she had no right to tell him how to do it.

Since that day, he'd had trouble sleeping. Her long, dark brown hair tied up in a low ponytail, her green eyes boring into his. She might be attractive, but she had no tact. So what if she had a trim and toned body to die for? He wasn't falling for that.

He stared at the screen, struggling to focus on his next words when someone tugged on his shoulder. He turned to see the short, stout form of his editor hovering over him. Fernando was thirty-five, five years older than him, but they got along well both personally and professionally. "How are you coming along with that article about Abel Lopez? We needed it yesterday, buddy." His friend rubbed his bushy eyebrows.

Rafael nodded. "It's coming along, but I have to get this right. His daughter hates me for tarnishing his name in the last article."

Fernando's eyes narrowed as he played with his stubble. "I hear you, but if we don't get this out today, it won't make production for the morning's edition. Get a move on, Rafael. We have other news stories to cover."

"If you leave me alone, I will get to it, Nando."

Fernando scoffed and put up his hand, directing his attention to a features editor sitting behind him. "I am coming, Alma. Do not miss my charming presence so soon." His friend was conventionally handsome, married with two children, but he liked to flirt with some of the female staff, and they tolerated it.

Blanca returned from the break room and sat at her desk, facing Rafael's. She looked radiant in her flowing, cotton dress. Love with Carlos showed. "Thanks for doing this article, Rafael. I'm sure Daniela will appreciate it. I hope you don't mind doing it, but it can repair things. Abel was a good man."

He turned to her and rested his back against his chair. "She'd better appreciate it. Otherwise, she'll have my head in a guillotine."

Blanca pulled out research notes from her drawer, placed them on to a document holder next to her screen and started typing. "Daniela's still hurting, so be kind. I imagine you're still questioning the source of those documents about the money?"

He stopped typing. "An anonymous source bothers me, Blanca, but it also checks out. Lopez appeared to embezzle the funds, but I don't know who the source is. It had to be someone working with him. I've asked around and no one at the company seems to know anything about who could have sent me those financial statements."

Blanca tilted her head, typing as she talked. "It is weird, that's for sure. But I imagine it's someone who has a reason for doing what he did. Either to ease his or her conscience, or because they hated Abel with a vengeance. It doesn't matter whether it turned out to be true or not."

Two hours later, Rafael finished his article and sent it to Fernando. "Done and dusted, Blanca. I can focus on something else now."

She gave him a thumbs up and squared her shoulders. "You should've let me read it first. Is it compassionate and balanced?"

He sighed. "Are you serious? I write facts, so no emotions, remember. But it paints him in a positive light. Tell your friend it'll be hot off the press tomorrow morning and she can read it." He clicked into his email. "What are you working on?"

"A woman's fight against a corporation that unfairly dismissed her at work. She has a great chance of getting compensated."

"That's good. If she has people on her side, then she might win. Otherwise, a lone person fighting an unfair dismissal can be next to impossible."

Rafael clicked on an email with an unusual subject: *Great article. Keep them coming.* But the body of the email was blank. Was this his source? He turned to his co-worker behind him. "Hey, Emilio. You're good with computers. Come here a second." Blanca watched him curiously but remained silent.

"Sure, dude." Emilio locked his computer and strutted over. He threaded his hands through his messy, blonde waves and towered over Rafael. "What's up?"

Rafael pointed at the email. "Can you trace who sent this email?" Rafael got up to let Emilio sit at his desk. The tall, solid man concentrated on the screen, clicking keys. Whatever he was doing made no sense to Rafael.

Some time later, Emilio shook his head. "I have tried a few things, but I haven't the faintest. Whoever sent this email is most likely using a VPN to hide his IP address. He could be using software that lets you send emails without registration. All they would've had to do is enter your address, the subject heading, and hit Send. No trace at all if you don't add your details."

Rafael's spine tightened. "Why would someone hide their identity?"

Emilio got up and touched him on the shoulder. "You have a fan, dude. Relish it, and don't over-think it." He headed back to his desk.

Blanca leaned closer. "Do you think it's the same guy who sent you those financial statements?"

He frowned. "It has to be, but why? Why are they doing this?" Rafael pressed a finger to his temple, fighting off a headache. "I wonder what they'll think of my next article about Abel Lopez. It's just the opposite and paints him in a positive way."

Blanca squinted. "I'm sure it's the last you'll hear from them. They got what they wanted and will most likely leave you alone."

"You're right. I am over-thinking this." He leaned back in his chair, staring hard at the screen as if it would provide insight. He wondered if there was another way to trace this email. The police might be able to, but they'd need probable cause. Shaking away his ruminations, he picked up a list of contacts to ring for his next article and thought nothing more about the email.

Chapter 6

BUSINESS LOSS

D aniela's ballet school in Madrid was only fifteen kilometres from her house. It was a small one-storey studio in an old, grey building she owned that had once been a house. Under the roof line, a row of small, timber-framed windows let in the light. Above the glass front doors hung a sign displaying the name of the school: *Asombrar La Escuele De Baile,* flanked by silhouettes of ballet poses. Across the road was a shopping strip with restaurants and cafes. A clothing boutique and shoe store stood on either side of her school, helping make it more visible within the community.

The school offered beginner, intermediate and advanced classical ballet, lyrical jazz, and contemporary dance classes to all dancers from the ages of five up to the professional stage at about eighteen. She had several dance teachers on her payroll, and business had been booming since a few of her students had been offered international scholarships to the most prestigious dance schools in several countries. The exposure of her popular dancers brought enrolments which she couldn't accommodate in her premises. As a result, she planned to secure a bigger building and expand her business.

Daniela thrived on the challenge of teaching young students ballet and other dance styles, setting budgets, managing her small staff and handling administrative tasks. She prided herself on moulding young dancers into professionals who could compete for awards.

She walked down a narrow corridor to her office. A few classes were already in session in the studios down the hall. The competence of her staff meant she didn't always need to be present to manage the studio.

She put down her dance bag, sat at her desk and flicked through a multitude of invoices she needed to send out for the next term of classes. She never had an office until recently, but the growth in the number of students had necessitated sectioning off a part of the dance room to create space for these administrative chores. Music and Sophia's loud instructions reverberated behind her. Checking the timetable displayed on the wall, she realised the class would end in five minutes.

Her phone buzzed in her bag. "Hello."

"Hello, Ms Lopez. This is Isabela's mum, Alicia. Sorry to call you so late, and I know you must be busy. But ... we ... we ... I mean, Isabela and I have decided to change dance schools. I am sorry."

Daniela cleared her throat. "What? Why is that?"

"Ahh, you see. We feel that her needs have changed, and she'd be better suited to another school nearby. I am sorry, but I won't be paying for classes for next term."

"This is all very sudden, Alicia. Is there something that Isabela wasn't happy about? How can I best serve her?"

"No, nothing like that, but you know how it is. Our needs have changed. I am sorry."

Daniela resigned herself to the situation. "If you're sure, but if you change your mind, Isabela is welcome back any time." She ended the call with a heavy heart, realising that she hadn't known that Isabela had been unhappy in class. Isabela had excelled and was on her way to winning huge competitions.

Sofia entered the office. "Oh, that was a great class. The girls were pumped." She wore black leotards, and her round face was flushed with excitement. Her buxom figure suited her soulful brown eyes. Her brown hair was tied up in a high bun. "Are you okay?"

She shrugged. "Isabela's mother just called. She's pulling her out to join another dance school. I thought she was happy."

Sofia sat on a chair opposite. "Strange. Did she mention why?"

Daniela shook her head. "Only that her needs have changed."

"Hmm. It happens, I guess. Don't you have quite a few on the waiting list, and what about the new building? Have you signed the lease yet?"

"Not yet. I am still debating between two locations, so I'm not sure." Her phone's buzzing again interrupted. "Hello." Her shoulders deflated as another parent pulled a student out of the school.

Sofia frowned. "Another one?" Daniela nodded. Her eyes looked into the distance. "I left a couple of messages for you." Sophia picked up two yellow sticky notes. "Two messages from another two students pulling out. I'm sorry." She took a breath. "Start calling those on the waiting list. I'm sure they'd be stoked to hear we have new openings in classical ballet."

Daniela nodded. "You're right. It does leave it open for them. Why do you always see the good in things, Sofia?"

She clasped her hands together and beamed. "What can I say? I am your favourite dance teacher, after all."

Daniela chuckled. "Do not let others hear you say that." She got up from her desk. "I've got a lyrical jazz class to teach now. I'll see you afterwards."

Sofia gave her a reassuring grin. "I've got my next one now, too."

Daniela wondered whether Rafael's article about her father had led to the cancellations. But as they headed towards their respective dance studios, Daniela's mood lifted. She greeted her students and began doing what she loved to do best. She could no longer be a professional dancer, but she could remain in the industry.

Gripping her dance bag tightly over her shoulder, Daniela crossed the car park after finishing dance classes and closing up. The night was warm and breezy as she nodded "good evening" to passers-by. The next day she planned to call the students on the top of her waiting list and invite them to join the school.

She heard a laugh behind her, but when she turned, she didn't see anyone. She continued and heard the laugh again, but once again saw no one when she turned back. Was she hearing things? *I must be more tired than I thought. I haven't been sleeping well since my father died.*

When she arrived home, she saw that the potted plant near the front door had been tampered with. Something was stuck into the soil. She pulled out a crossword puzzle. What was this? Was someone playing some type of game? If her father hadn't died, she would have thought it was him visiting, as he had loved puzzles just as much as she did.

Her blood turned cold when she remembered the police officer telling her that they had found a crossword puzzle beside her father's body. But until they got the autopsy results, she wouldn't speculate that her father's death was suspicious. Then again, it might have been someone who knew the circumstances of her father's death. She didn't remember the police releasing that information to the public. Who else knew about her love of crossword puzzles?

Daniela remembered that Blanca was out with Carlos tonight, and she vowed to tell her about this invasion as soon as she got home. Goosebumps spread over her skin as she looked over her shoulder, scanning the nearby area. With her back to the door, she took a breath and gazed out into the street. This had to be a silly prank. Turning back to the door, she unlocked it quickly and slammed it behind her. She would not let this spook her.

Chapter 7

A MESSAGE

Rafael and Fernando puffed along on side-by-side treadmills, staring through the windows at a shopping precinct.

Working out was the best way Rafael knew to release tension whenever he felt like he was losing control. His goal reached, he stopped the treadmill. Sweat dripped down his body as he picked up his towel and wiped his face and the back of his neck. He gulped water from his bottle, savouring its coolness, then picked up a pair of dumbbells. His biceps flexed under his damp t-shirt as he alternately raised and lowered the weights for twenty counts on each side, then sighed with relief. He hated the gym, but the physical rewards afterwards paid off.

Fernando hit him on the shoulder. "You jerk. Why do you have to look so great compared to me? I can't seem to lose any weight."

Rafael chuckled. "Well, if you stop eating those hot snacks late at night, you might lose a few kilos."

Fernando scoffed. "Tell me that when you've got your own wife who takes care of your every need. She's a great cook; what can I say?"

"Don't complain then, Nando. Embrace it."

They made their way outside to Rafael's car when he spotted a piece of paper stuck underneath one of his windscreen wipers. "What's this?" Fernando shrugged. He pulled it out and stared numbly at the typewritten words: "TRASHY NEWS STORY."

Rafael bit his bottom lip and stroked his damp air. He turned to his friend. "This fan of mine is doing my head in, Nando. I got that email about my last article, and now this. I assume they're referring to my latest article."

Fernando knit his brows. "The article about Abel Lopez, you mean?" Rafael nodded. "They must hate the guy. Your latest one was a glowing profile of him being a family man and overcoming alcohol." He fixed his gaze on the note. "So, someone who hates Abel hates you now?"

Rafael rubbed his chin. Who was this guy? "I am assuming that whoever sent me those financial reports is the same person. What do I do with this?" He opened the driver's door and placed the paper in the back seat. "What do I do?"

Fernando got in the passenger side. "I'd say this is bordering on harassment, so you need to take this to the police, Rafael. Get this on record."

"But surely now that I've stopped writing about Abel, it'll be all good? Whatever else I write will be irrelevant, won't it?"

"Possibly, depending on his reason for doing this," Fernando said. "It's up to you what you want to do, but if it was me, I'd take it to the police." He rubbed his hands. "Or you could wait and see if this happens again. But keep that piece of paper just in case, and document everything strange that happens. Times, dates, incidents. Keep a record of everything."

Rafael started the motor. "I might need to dig deeper into Abel's life if I want answers. It sounds like he had an enemy."

"Just leave it alone, Raf. Focus on your job. You don't have any time to go researching stuff that's not about your work. Don't I give you enough to do? Just say the word and I'll pile more on until the new year."

He shook his head. "Don't you dare. I do have a life too, you know."

Fernando smirked. "What life? Work is your life, Raf. Don't mess that up. I like how you're always my most efficient and fastest reporter. Keep it up. More awards will have your name on them. If Abel Lopez's death was a crime, my police contact will let me know about it. The police might hold a press conference if Lopez was murdered. You can write about the suspicious death once we know what we're dealing with. But then again, he might have died of natural causes. In that case, there'll be nothing to write about."

Rafael dropped off his friend and waved goodbye, heading to his own house. Stepping inside, he dropped his gym bag on the floor and poured himself a glass of water. He noticed that the sliding door in the living room to the patio was partially open. He was sure he had closed the door before he left for the gym.

He closed the door and turned on the large TV. After flicking through channels, he got bored, so went to hit the shower.

He thought about Abel Lopez. The man had left his wife and two daughters behind six years ago—why? He had quit drinking and appeared to have loved his family, so what had caused him to leave without a word? Rafael could understand if he no longer loved his wife and wanted a divorce, but he would still want to see his daughters. It seemed to be out of character to break off all ties. Something had made him leave, but what?

Chapter 8

CHANCE MEETING

"I want to see an *Assemble*." Daniela clasped her hands together and roamed the room, watching and critiquing the thirteen-year-old girls. "Alma and Augustina, I don't see you landing on two feet. Try again. And remember your posture, ladies."

Briefly, Daniela admired the colourful butterfly wallpaper, put up by the previous owner of the building. Then she re-focused on her class. "Now, I'd like to see a *Jete Battu*. Let's see that extra beat." Daniela lifted her shoulders. "I want a *Jete* and a *Grand Jete*. Make that leap, and always remember your posture and breathing. Keep up the pace, Alma. We have competitions coming up, and these moves are critical. You have a chance to win, and win big. Maybe a scholarship." As Alma flowed into the same rhythm as the group, she nodded, satisfied that the girl was performing well. "Take a couple of minutes and grab a drink." Daniela waited until the girls drank from their water bottles and resumed their positions.

Clasping her hands, she said, "Now let's try a *Retire Devant* at the barre. Remember to bend those knees." Feet pitter-pattered to the barre. "Remember, the toe needs to be directly in front of the knee."

She gave them a minute. "Now let's practice the *Retire Derriere*, and for those of you who forget; this move is the toe behind the knee." Daniela took a breath and watched as Sofia hovered near the door with a man. Was he one of the fathers picking up his daughter? She scrutinized the girls as she made her way alongside the barre. "Good. Very good. Much improved posture." She took a breath. "That will be all for tonight, ladies. Great lesson. I'll see you all next week."

The girls picked up their bags, smiled, waved and rushed out. Sofia came in with the man behind her. His shoulder-length hair looked glossy and his bulky frame made her wonder if he could simply touch someone and make them fall. "Hey, Daniela. This is my cousin, Diego. He's down here from Barcelona and wanted to meet the famous ballet dancer and owner of the popular dance school."

He smiled, and Daniela noticed his braces. She shook his offered hand. It was warm. "Such a pleasure to meet a celebrity. I am a fan of your work," he said. "I have nieces who love dancing and they've read about your time as a professional dancer. Sorry you had to stop." He turned to look at the room. "And this place is amazing. Quite an achievement."

"Thank you, Diego. I travelled to Barcelona as a dancer, and I must say it's a magical place. I will have to get back there one day."

"It is that. So how long have you owned this school?"

"A couple of years now, and it's going strong. What brings you to Madrid?"

He had a nice smile. "I wanted to see my cousin, but I also have an engineering conference here. I plan to extend my stay beyond the conference. It's not often I get to see my beautiful cousin."

Sofia prodded him by the hand. "I'm ready to go now, Diego."

He smiled at her. "Let's have a coffee with Daniela. I am in the presence of royalty here. My friends' children are fans of your work, too."

Sofia frowned. "I am exhausted, Diego. Can't we do it another night?"

He touched her playfully on the shoulder. "Oh, don't be such a party-pooper, cousin. Just one night. Who knows if I'll be back here?" He watched Daniela with curiosity. "Unless you disagree, Daniela."

She didn't want to appear rude, and he had charm. "Okay. One coffee is fine. Sofia, you and I haven't gone out in a while. It'll be an early night."

Sofia nodded. "Fine, but let's make it quick."

Daniela locked up for the night, and they went to a coffee shop across the road. A shelf of potted plants and a large counter took up half of the space. Smells of fresh coffee and cinnamon permeated the air, and the laughter and loud voices gave the cafe a friendly and easy-going vibe.

Stepping in, Daniela saw a familiar figure sitting in a corner. *No, it can't be. What is Rafael Martin doing in this area?* She put her head down, hoping he wouldn't see her, and didn't dare look up again in case he spotted her. They headed to a shiny table and sat down on brown-padded stools. She just hoped that Rafael didn't see her behind another group of people alongside the rows of tables.

"I will go order us coffee," said Diego.

Rafael clenched his fists in a corner chair, sipping his hot chocolate. He was sitting where Daniela couldn't see him, but he wanted to approach her until he noticed a handsome young man ogling her. He had ordered them coffee and the waiter had now just handed them their drinks.

Rafael lost count of how many times the handsome guy laughed in her direction or touched her shoulder. Daniela seemed to shine in his company. Why did he care? He didn't know the woman.

He had wanted to visit her school and talk to her about the latest article he had written about her father. Blanca had advised him to catch up with her to apologise again and get her thoughts on the latest article. But when he'd arrived at the dance school, it was already closed, so he decided to have a coffee. He did not expect to see Daniela here.

The dance attire she wore made her look young and free, as if she glowed in it. Not that he cared. He had to make the effort to approach her and apologise again. He didn't like people being angry with him. He had to make this right.

A voice broke his reverie. "What are you doing here?"

He looked up to see Daniela standing with her arms crossed as if she wanted him to leave. "Hello. Last I checked, this cafe was free for all to attend."

She glared. "Are you following me? This place is near my dance school."

"No, I was in the area. But while you're here, I wanted to apologise again for that article. Did you read the latest one about your father's good deeds?"

She nodded. "It was okay, I guess. But what you did was still insensitive."

He licked his lips, noticing the cleavage visible in her short top. Her short, tight skirt showed off her well-toned feminine curves. Her lipstick was smudged, and her eyes glistened underneath the low lighting. "So, who are you with?"

"Not that it's any of your business, but the lady is a friend and one of my dance teachers. Diego is her cousin down here from Barcelona. He said you were staring from your table and I had to tell him I knew you. He then forced me to come over. Otherwise, I wouldn't have bothered." She squinted. "Why are you here?"

He smiled. "Can't a man enjoy a cup of coffee in his down time?"

She scoffed. "Your type always has a motive for everything they do." Her hands touched the base of her throat and she pressed her lips together.

"Why don't you take a seat. I wanted to talk to you. I can do an article to promote your dance school. What do you think?"

She shook her head. "I do just fine without your articles, thank you. Now if you'll excuse me, I'm off to the bathroom." She stormed off without waiting for a reply.

Why did she look even more beautiful when she was angry? He must be out of his mind. Just because she was attractive didn't mean he had to notice.

Chapter 9

AUTOPSY RESULTS

R afael left the court after hearing the ruling that Abel Lopez's sudden death was due to a heart attack. He wondered what could have prompted it. The man had no history of heart disease and didn't take any medication for his heart. How could a healthy man die so suddenly? Rafael felt there was something more here.

He returned to the newspaper office, where Emilio gave him a thumbs-up greeting as he fiddled with the lever on the side of his ergonomic chair. "How are you doing, dude? Heard you got the news about that suspicious death."

"I did. Not suspicious. Apparently, the guy died of a heart attack." Rafael waved to Blanca and the other staff members, then concentrated on his next article. *Coroner Rules Abel Lopez's Death As Not Suspicious,* he typed. He wondered whether his source would hate this new article, too. Would he get another message on his windscreen from someone who professed to be judge and jury?

Rafael didn't care; he was just doing his job. If Daniela didn't like this article, it was her problem. He had a job to do and would only present the facts.

Blanca stopped typing, staring hard at her screen as if in deep thought. "I'm having writer's block."

He tilted his head. "Strange. You never have writer's block. Is everything okay?"

She nodded. "Sure. Why wouldn't it be? Just tired, that's all."

Rafael watched her closely and noticed her hands shaking. Something was wrong, but he wouldn't push it for now. Did it have something to do with Daniela?

Daniela rang her mother's doorbell, anxious to hear the autopsy results. As she waited on the doorstep, she felt a chill in her back.

Eva swung open the door. "Hi Daniela." She hugged her sister. When they pulled apart, Eva's blue eye assessed her warmly. In spite of having one glass eye, her other senses were sharp. She drew a hand through her long, glossy brown hair which flowed down to her lower back in waves. "It's so good to see you again. Can I make you a nice cup of tea? Or would you prefer a cold drink?"

"No thanks, Eva. I'm fine. Where's Mum?"

Eva frowned as they sat on the couch. "She's naturally upset after reading the autopsy report online. It brought everything back."

Daniela nodded. "I haven't checked the findings online yet. What does it say?" The truth was, she didn't have the courage to check the coroner's findings without her family. "Please just sum it up for me. I'll read it later."

Eva stared into her lap, then lifted her gaze to Daniela. "They ruled it as not suspicious, saying he'd had a heart attack during the night."

Daniela breathed a sigh of relief that it wasn't suspicious, but why did something not feel right? Her shoulders tightened and she dug her nails into her hands. "Did he have heart problems?"

Eva's eyes became wet. "No, he didn't. But sometimes people just die of sudden heart attacks. It happens."

Daniela stared into her hands. "If we only knew what he'd been up to in the last six years, we'd know if he had some kind of stress that might have caused this."

"I don't know, Daniela. At least he didn't remarry. The police mentioned he was a loner and didn't see anyone. I cannot believe he just died alone. With no one. And why did he leave us when things were so good after he stopped drinking?"

Daniela wrapped her arms around her sister, stroking the back of her head. "I wish I knew, but maybe we'll find out. For now, we have to be there for Mum." They pulled apart and Daniela gave her sister a reassuring smile.

The shuffling of feet alerted her to her mother coming in. "Hello, dear." She kissed Daniela on the cheek. Her black hair seemed to have more grey in it today, and she moved over to the armchair and slouched. "I am sorry I wasn't here. I'm not feeling the best." She gazed into the distance. "I take it you heard the news about your father?"

"I did, and I'm sorry Mum. Do you know if he ever had heart problems?"

She shook her head. "Not when he lived with us, but maybe he just burned himself out. I don't know, dear. He didn't deserve to die alone like this."

"No, he didn't, but you know the newspapers will be printing this information. Are you ready for it?"

Her mother nodded. "Of course. It's what must be done. They report the news and your father became famous after what he ..."

"I still find that a bit strange, Mum. Why would he embezzle money when he had a good salary as a financial analyst? It just doesn't make sense."

"I guess we will never know, darling. What I find strange, too, is why he became a hermit these last six years. When he was home, he was always catching up with friends, and loved having visitors over. He must have alienated everyone."

Eva looked pensive. "Maybe his financial crimes made him that way."

Daniela shook her head. "It's possible, I guess."

An hour later, Daniela left her mother's home. In her car, she leaned back against the seat and tried to put the facts together. Her father had left them six years earlier, after which he became a hermit and embezzled funds from his company. He didn't have heart problems, but he died of a heart attack. There were so many unanswered questions. It was like solving a crossword puzzle.

As she turned on the motor, she saw something on the passenger seat. A crossword puzzle lay open, scattered words highlighted in yellow: *Let The Games Begin*. What was this?

Chapter 10

THE FUNERAL

Daniela wiped away her tears as she sat in the front pew, listening to the priest deliver his sermon about her father: Abel, who was a kind family man who contributed to the community, but made mistakes along the way. It seemed strange to put embezzlement down as a mistake, but he couldn't say otherwise in church.

Daniela sat between her mother and sister, with Blanca, Carlos, and Kim behind them. A few other family members and friends attended, including Sofia and her other dance teachers.

Her eyes roamed the church. Murals and paintings on the ceilings and walls represented the Renaissance period. Brown timber pews stood in rows and lined the walls. Lights suspended from the ceiling and candles in stands and sconces lit the space. A large painting hung at the back of the altar.

Daniela took a breath as she stepped up to the podium to deliver the eulogy. Looking at the gathering, she gasped at seeing Rafael in the back. What was he doing here?

She hadn't wanted to give the eulogy, but her mother had insisted. She believed that despite leaving his family, Abel had been a good man and the eulogy should focus on his good points, leaving out the bad.

Daniela refocused on the eulogy, "My father was a man of honour who provided for his family." She pushed back tears. "I remember a time when he had taken us to the beach and threw me in the water. He pretended to be a shark and raced after me. Eva and I were in fits of laughter and found it hard to get away from him. He was too fast and a good swimmer. We cherished those trips." Her heart warmed. "Another time, I remember I had a hard time with a teacher. I came home and he listened when I told him how she had screamed at me for not finishing my homework. My father listened without judgement. Then he dried my tears with a gentle hand and wrapped his arms around me." She took a breath and remembered the times he had been drunk or had lost his job; that was a different story. She spoke about other memories with pride, and realised they'd had more good memories than bad. Fighting back tears, she pushed on. "My father made mistakes along the way, but he moved on from that, and we all still love him, and always will." Clearing her throat, she rubbed a fresh tear and made her way back to her seat.

Then her mother lit a huge candle, and the pallbearers carried out the coffin. Daniela couldn't stop the rush of tears as a slow Latin ballad played in the room. One by one, the guests emptied the pews and walked out into the wind. Daniela joined her family to accept condolences from the guests.

Daniela faced her mother. "Are you okay?"

Her mother nodded. "I will be, darling." She held her daughter's hand while Eva touched her shoulder on the other side.

Eva looked into her eyes. She always thought her sister was beautiful with her long, brown flowing hair. "The eulogy was beautiful, Dani. Thank you for doing that. I love you, sis."

Daniela's breathing slowed as she leaned in. "I love you too, Eva." She straightened her posture as the guests hugged and kissed her on the cheek. One by one, they gave their reassuring smiles and nodded in understanding until Rafael approached.

"I am so sorry for your loss, Daniela." He kissed her on both cheeks and the tingle down her spine brought her back to the present.

Play nice! This was her father's funeral, and she felt emotional today and not herself. The tingle was just nerves. "Thank you." She assumed he attended the funeral out of obligation after the articles he wrote. He nodded, his gaze fixed on her as he moved towards her mother.

Daniela's legs felt unsteady and weak as she walked to the cemetery. By the time the coffin was lowered into the ground, she let the tears stream down her cheeks. She threw roses onto the coffin, and as she returned to her position in the front row, she saw someone in the distance. A man wearing dark glasses and a long coat watched the burial. Who was he and why didn't he join the ceremony?

After the priest finished praying Daniela turned back around, but the man was no longer there. *Strange!* She didn't have the desire nor the energy to worry about someone who was too anxious to attend. It could have been another reporter for all she knew.

Back at her mother's house, Daniela rushed to serve warm and cold savouries and snacks. Eva gave glasses of Spanish sherry to standing guests in the living room and in the backyard. Blanca and Kim helped pass around trays of food.

Moving outside, Daniela felt her heart skip a beat to see Rafael whispering to Carlos. "Would you guys like anything?"

Rafael chose a ham baguette. "Thank you."

Carlos gave her a reassuring smile and took a cheesy croquette. "It was a beautiful service. How are you doing, Daniela?"

"Surviving, Carlos. Surviving." She moved to other guests until she put the tray on a buffet table. As she was about to head inside, Rafael rushed to her side. Where was Carlos? He must have gone inside.

"I wanted you to know that your mother invited me today. She spoke to Carlos and he passed on the message. Carlos and I are friends, and I don't want you to think I gate-crashed."

Her chest tightened. "Why would my mother invite you?"

"She liked the article I wrote about your father, and I wanted to give my condolences, too. I am sorry if you hate me, but I can only say sorry so many times." He looked around. "Can I get you anything to eat or drink?"

She shook her head. "No, I'm fine. I really should go inside and see what else needs to be done." Her breathing was erratic and she felt sweat around her neck.

"Please wait. Just a few minutes. Carlos is helping out, so there is a group inside that can give you a break."

Daniela smelled his musky, heady scent. His black pants and crimson shirt brought out his eyes and enhanced his looks. But he was still a reporter who had tarnished her father's name. Was she being too hard on him? She was still grieving after all and wasn't thinking straight. "What could we possibly talk about?"

Rafael fixed his gaze on her. "You and your family seem close."

"We are close." She remembered his article about the autopsy results. "I must say your article about my dad's autopsy results was tasteful. And thank you for saying honourable things about him in your second article. I appreciate that."

He nodded. "Thank you. Like I said, I only report facts, and your father seemed to be a good man with heart. How's your family coping with all this?"

Daniela didn't have the energy to converse with this man, nor get personal with him. "Listen, I can't do this right now. I have to go."

His eyes darkened. "Of course. I'm sorry."

She rushed inside the house, her face flushed and her hands sweaty. Wiping away the dampness behind her neck, she headed into the bathroom, closed the door, and bowed her head over the basin. Hands shaking, she bent down to wash her face. An image of Rafael's sad eyes flashed before her. All she knew was that she needed to get her bearings before facing the guests.

Chapter II

TELEPHONE CALLS

A week after the funeral, Daniela took Kim's yoga class. Balancing on one leg, she raised her arms straight out from her chest, then pointed her hands upwards in a tree position. Her right foot leaned into her opposite leg in a triangular position while she took slow, calming breaths. She almost toppled, but kept her balance.

At the front of the class, Kim pressed her palms together, her unblemished olive skin not even breaking a sweat. "That's it, ladies. I will see you next week."

The women surrounding Daniela in the yoga centre grabbed their mats and wandered off, shouting goodbyes to Kim. Her friend's eyes lit up as she waved to them. Kim took pride in helping others, finding spiritual purpose and strategies to relax from her Chinese culture and spiritual way of being.

Daniela picked up her mat and looked around the yoga centre. A large window admitted sunlight and gave a view of the centre of Madrid. The floor gleamed. Posters of the Buddha and meditative poses lined the walls behind her. Other posters displayed affirmations in all colours on the wall, and a small kitchen area in the back ensured Kim took well-earned breaks.

Her phone rang in her bag. The screen showed an unfamiliar number. She pressed the button. "Hello." Silence. "Hello. Is anyone there? Hello." A faint sound of breathing was all she heard until the call disconnected. *Probably just a wrong number.*

Throwing the bag's strap over her shoulder, she faced Kim who ushered her over to the kitchenette. Kim took out a bottle of Cava sparkling wine from the fridge.

"Isn't it a bit early for wine?"

Kim picked up two wine glasses from an overhead cupboard, poured the wine with a firm hand, and handed her a glass. "It looks like you need this after the funeral. Why don't you catch me up on what is going on?"

"What do you mean, girl?"

Kim brought her hands together and looked away. "I hear things from Blanca, but not you. You can tell me anything, Daniela. I am here for you, night and day. I want to help in any way I can. Don't shut me out."

Daniela leaned forward and gave her a reassuring smile. "Oh, Kim, my girl. I live with Blanca, so I tell her things. It's been busy lately, so I forget what's been going on."

Kim nodded then sighed. She played with a strand of her hair. "I understand that, but before the funeral, you didn't tell me about the potted plant in front of your home. The one with a crossword puzzle buried inside it. That is strange, and you should have told me. I want to be there for you if you are being harassed. Who would do that?"

Daniela sipped her wine. "I'm sorry, but I'm sure it was a prankster who knew my dad loved crossword puzzles. I think it was just meant as a joke, nothing serious."

Kim stared at her strangely. "Do you think it could have been one of your father's clients?" She played with her long hair, her eyes shifting.

"Oh, God! I hope not. That's all I need. My father's mistakes interfering with my life. Not when I've got the dance school and my good reputation to maintain."

Kim squeezed her shoulder. "I am sorry. I didn't mean to put that in your head. You are probably right. It has to be a poor joke, that's all. Someone who knew your dad loved crossword puzzles as you do."

Five minutes later, Blanca walked in, staring at her phone. She sat beside Kim, across from Daniela. "Hello, ladies." Blanca put her phone aside. "I'm here for Kim's next yoga session. Sorry I missed the earlier one, but while you're here, I wanted to ask about doing the promotional piece on your business. Let's lock in a date and we'll do a quick interview. Carlos has agreed to do photography, too."

"I am sure the promotion will help, after everything that's happened with your father," Kim agreed. "How many students have you lost now?"

Daniela shrugged. "Ballpark, around ten or so. It must be about my father, but the mothers are not going to tell me that to my face. I have to live with it for now, but hopefully it'll pass. So much for wanting to expand the business. The timing's not right, not when my dad's crime has changed all that." She swallowed. "I need to make sure I stay afloat. Any promotional articles could be a lifesaver. I could set people straight by telling them I am not my father and explain how he wasn't a part of my life for six years."

Blanca turned to Daniela. "How about you meet me for lunch next week and I'll start the interview then. Maybe after I finish work, I can come by with Carlos and ask you a few more questions. We could get testimonials from some of the students and tell them how wonderful, smart, and generous you are."

Daniela's heart lifted. "Thanks, Blanca. I'll put out a notice to parents about testimonials. I assume these testimonials will go in your article. Is your boss okay with this? I mean, don't you have more important articles to write? Actual news?"

Blanca nodded. "I've asked my boss already, and anything that will sell more papers, he's happy with. It's a numbers game and good business sense. The mystery of your father and the innocent daughter."

Daniela shifted in her seat, sipping her wine until she finished it. "I have to tell you something." Blanca and Kim leaned forward, concern in their eyes. "I got into my car after visiting my mum to talk about the autopsy results. I found a crossword puzzle on the passenger seat of the car, and it wasn't there before." Her friends' eyes widened. "And I wouldn't normally worry about this, but earlier today, I got a call and no one was there. All I heard was breathing."

Blanca took a breath. "Jesus, Dani. What is going on here? Are these enemies of your father? Are you sure you didn't leave that puzzle in your car? You might have forgotten."

Kim nodded. "Agreed. It could have been your puzzle. You're always indulging in them. And people misdial all the time." She didn't sound convincing.

Daniela got up and kissed her cheek. "I don't want you guys to worry, but I thought I should at least tell you what's been happening. I know you have your next session and I've got to go." She turned to Blanca and kissed her. "I'll see you tonight, and Kim, we'll talk soon."

"Wait," Blanca protested. "Let's finish talking about this, Dani. Don't go yet."

Kim shook her head. "Daniela, please stay for the next session and then we'll talk. You can't just drop a bombshell on us and leave like that."

She blew them both a kiss. "I love you guys. See you, ladies."

Daniela left. In her car, she realised she'd forgotten to tell the police about the crossword puzzle in her car. Shouldn't it be checked for fingerprints? She doubted it would have any, and besides, she might have forgotten about putting it in her car. She'd had a lot on her mind recently. Even if someone else had put it there, there was no evidence that her car had been broken into.

Her phone rang, jolting her out of her reverie. Again, the display showed an unknown number.

When she answered, more out of curiosity than anything else, she heard muffled laughter. "Who is this?" She waited with bated breath but whoever it was hung up. What was going on, and who was doing this to her?

Chapter 12

MARKETING A BUSINESS

R afael typed his last word into an article about a series of
robberies occurring in the city of Salamanca, as Julieta, his co-
worker and web reporter, nudged him. She had bright, red hair cut in
a bob-style.

"Can you send me that article and I'll get the digital version
organised." Her blue eyes fixed on his. She touched the base of her
throat. "Oh, and now would be good. You always take hours to give
me your articles."

"Happy to, Jules." He sent his article to her inbox. "Done."

She nodded. "Thank you, Mr. Martin. You're free to carry on with
your other work."

He looked towards the newsroom door and wondered when
Blanca would return from lunch. She had mentioned meeting Daniela
at a cafe close by, and he wanted to hear how Daniela was coping. She
should be back by now, but it remained quiet.

Brushing away thoughts of Daniela, he noticed a message from an
unknown sender. The subject heading said, *Your Article Did The Job
This Time*. Was he talking about the autopsy results, and how did it

do the job exactly? By reporting the facts or not? The empty body of the email didn't surprise him. That was like the previous email.

What was he supposed to do with these emails? Emilio couldn't find the source, so should he show them to the police? Or dismiss them? It wasn't like these emails were a crime or had threatened him in any way. Surely now that he would no longer be writing about Abel Lopez, these messages should stop?

Nodding, he decided. As of this moment, these emails would have to stop. He would focus on different matters now.

"Hey, Rafael. I'm back, and I bring company," said Blanca.

His heart skipped a beat as he saw Daniela blush. She gave him a brief wave, and he wondered if his charm was working on her. She looked breathtaking in her translucent white linen shirt and short, black skirt. "Hello, Daniela. How was lunch?"

"Fine, thanks," Daniela said.

"We had tacos and they were delicious," Blanca said as if to make up for Daniela's brief response. "You should try that place some time. Such a treat." Her eyes roamed. "Is Fernando in his office? I need to talk to him about that article I'm writing about Daniela's dance school."

Rafael nodded. "He should be."

Blanca beamed. "We'll be back." As they headed towards Fernando's office, Daniela looked over her shoulder briefly.

His mind went blank as he tried to remember his next priority. He opened a list of contacts for his follow-up article on the robbery. He started calling and setting up interviews with his police contacts and a witness, adding the appointments to his online calendar.

When Blanca and Daniela returned, they brought Fernando with them. Blanca looked disappointed and held Daniela's shoulder. What was going on?

"Listen, man," Fernando began. "Would you mind wrapping up that robbery article, or I can give you one extra day to finish it. I need you to do this promotional piece for Daniela's business. Blanca's had a request from management. They want her to go to Valencia tonight to interview people about a corrupt corporation. She'll be gone for at least a week, but Daniela needs this promotional piece to be done pronto. She's losing a lot of students and business because of what's happened with her father, and we need to help her."

Daniela put up her hand. "It is fine if he can't do it. I can find someone else to promote my business. No problem."

Blanca sighed. "I am so sorry, Daniela. I have been working on this corruption story, so management requested me. But Rafael will do an even better job than me on your marketing. Let him do it."

Fernando slapped him on the shoulder. "Rafael can do several articles simultaneously in his sleep. He'll do an amazing job. Let us handle it, Daniela."

Rafael's gaze lingered on Daniela, whose fingers played with her palms. "I am happy to do it, and we can meet up at your school tonight if you're free."

Daniela's eyes turned a shade darker. "I really don't need this article. In fact, I can wait for Blanca to return. I'm sure a week won't make much of a difference."

Blanca nudged Daniela. "Listen, girl. You need to make people listen, and in this piece they will listen. They need to know the real you, and not mistake you for your father. You've got to set the public straight and defend your honour."

What was Daniela's problem, Rafael wondered. It wasn't a big deal to write an article about her business. As Fernando mentioned, he could do it in his sleep. He wished she had more faith in his abilities, especially when she had her reputation to protect.

Ignoring his co-workers' eyes on them, he put up his hand. "I am happy to do this article because I like to keep busy. I'm ambitious, remember. A week is too long to wait, so let me do this for you. Let me set the public straight and promote not only you, but the business. It's a win-win scenario."

Daniela let out a small breath. "Fine. You can come to the school tonight at six o'clock. Don't be late. Carlos will be meeting us there for photographs."

He hid his excitement at the idea of getting to know Daniela. She was a way into writing new and interesting articles. That was all it was. He didn't need to think about Daniela being different from other women. He had had too many ex-girlfriends either cheat on him or break up with him, telling him he was married to his job. But he wasn't. He just didn't trust easily, and those women never gave him a reason to trust them. Putting his thoughts aside, he said, "Good. See you then." She waved to the others and headed to the exit. He watched the curved outline of her waist and the tanned muscles of her legs as she walked to the exit. No, he didn't need to think of her at all. This was just business, pure and simple.

Chapter 13

SHADOWING

R afael jotted down notes as he watched Daniela glide across the room, teaching ballet to young teenage girls. The red leotard she wore hugged her body, and her well-shaped legs looked as if they went on for miles. Her whole body was well-proportioned and feminine, and he had to look away to focus on the session. He didn't need any distractions.

He spoke into a small voice recorder. The way she showed her poise and confidence. Her posture was straight, and her eyes roamed the room as she picked up on dancer's weaknesses and explored their strengths.

Carlos had come earlier to take photographs of the school and dancers, and he secured a few testimonials to add as captions to the visuals. He promised to send Rafael the photos and testimonials to add to the newspaper article.

"Bend that knee, Luciana. Straighten your posture. Now focus. The exams are coming up, and despite the focus on progressive styles, you still need to perfect the technical aspects." She clasped her hands and walked around the room, circling the ten dancers in their leotards and ballet shoes. "Okay. Now, let's focus on the important aspects of ballet." She took a breath and looked at him with curiosity. He wondered what was going through her mind. "Okay, give me *Plier*." Her eyes wandered. "Good. Do it a few more times." She kept wandering around the room and reciting their flaws and strengths. "Show me *Etendre*. Luciana, stretch it out." She nodded. "Good. Don't forget to breathe with each move. That's important." She smiled at a few students. "Now give me the *Relever* and the *Sauter*, one after another." As she neared him, she clasped her hands together and focused on the movements. "Now the *Tourner*." She nodded. "Good. Let's do that a few more times." She waited and watched. "Now, the *Glisser*." She had a nice smile as he watched her work the room and scrutinise the dancers' moves. "Finally, the *Elancer*." She beamed again. "Excellent. Great work, ladies. I'll see you next week. For those of you who have a safe space at home, keep up the practice."

The girls smiled and waved to Daniela then rushed out, passing him on their way. Daniela approached with a nervous smile. "I know you must have been bored, but you wanted to see a live session."

Her fruity scent combined with sweat drew Rafael like a magnet. He was almost at a loss for words. "Ahh. No, not at all. It was interesting, and you certainly know how to teach well. Very disciplined, committed, and focused."

Daniela blushed. "Thank you. Now, I assume we're doing the interview?" He nodded. "Come into my office."

Daniela moved two chairs to the side of her desk and crossed her legs. Aware of the proximity of her body, he forced himself to look away. A small white heater stood in the corner but would not be used now in the summer. "Shoot. Ask your questions."

Rafael took out the recorder. "Can I record this so I'm more fully present?"

"Sure, why not?"

He cleared his throat. "Tell me about the age groups you teach here."

Daniela clasped her hands. "They're from the ages of five to eighteen. A few of our students have won scholarships and gone on to professional careers."

His heart warmed. "That is quite an achievement." He couldn't stop staring at her, and she looked away. "Can you tell me about the history of the school and your goals for the future, in terms of expansion or anything else." Rafael listened with a keen ear as she gave him her spiel. A knock interrupted. The dance teacher and that man from the cafe stood at the door. Rafael couldn't remember their names.

Daniela frowned. "Hey, Sofia. And good to see you again, Diego." She pointed to him. "This is Rafael, here to do the article on the school. Sofia's one of my best dance teachers, and this is Diego, her cousin, from Barcelona. He's visiting for a while."

Rafael rose and shook their hands. "Good to meet you both."

Diego's eyes lit up. "And it is great to see you writing about greatness here. Daniela is very popular with my nieces and friends' children. They watch her famous dance performances on social media all the time."

Rafael thrust his chest out. "I will do my best to paint her in the very best light, Diego. Thank you."

Sofia grinned. "That's great, Rafael." She faced Daniela. "Listen, I'm heading off, but I will see you tomorrow night. Is there anything else I need to do before I leave?"

She shook her head. "No, thanks Sofia. You can go. I'll see you tomorrow. Bye, Diego. And thank you for the flattery, but it's a gross exaggeration."

Diego leaned forward. "Of course it isn't. It was a pleasure to see you again, Daniela. And great to meet you, Rafael. These ladies have true talent."

"They do," he replied. This guy was definitely a ladies' man, and the way he stared at Daniela made him feel something close to jealousy. Was he trying to make a move on her? Not that he cared. Or did he?

Once they left, Rafael turned to her again. "So, before we got interrupted, you were about to tell me about your goals for the school."

"I am hoping to lease a larger building to accommodate all the students who want to come, and eventually buy it. I also want to look into bringing in investors so I can expand the school into other areas of Spain. I have started a special program for disadvantaged students who cannot afford my regular fees. I have managed to get some funding for this, and I'm hoping to expand this to other areas of Spain, too."

Rafael was tongue-tied as he took in the way she cared about people and had the biggest heart he knew. "That is commendable, Daniela. I don't know many people who would do what you're doing." He shifted focus. "And tell me about your days as a professional dancer. What happened?"

She took a breath. "At twenty-two years old, I injured my ankle while I was dancing." Knitting her brows, she continued. "I'd been dancing professionally for about four years. The roof leaked during a rainstorm, making the stage slippery." Daniela crossed her arms. "I remember the doctor telling me that my ankle wouldn't heal to its normal capacity, and despite training, I wouldn't be able to keep up the pace of a professional dancer. I didn't believe him, and I danced too soon and re-injured my ankle. I made it worse. It healed again, but I had no choice but to stop performing professionally." She beamed. "I love to teach, and I get that reward when others make it to that professional stage."

"It must have been hard to give up your dream."

She nodded, her eyes peering past him. "I struggled with it at first, but then I realised it was a blessing in disguise. I lost interest in the gruelling schedule of travel and performances and got to focus on teaching. I wanted to settle in one place, and I still do the occasional dance performance around Madrid. I don't mind doing that."

Rafael nodded. "It seems to have worked out well for you. You're a hit. Now, we need to focus on your father and how you haven't had contact with him for six years. That you had no idea about his actions. We need to maintain your reputation."

Daniela got up and opened a small fridge in the corner. "I have churros we can eat, and I can make us a hot chocolate with the press of a button." Rafael nodded, and she put two paper cups underneath her coffee machine. She handed one to Rafael with sachets of sugar. She put a tray of churros, a tub of chocolate, and a pile of napkins on the table.

Rafael bit into the churro then wiped his mouth with the napkin. "I imagine you must have been relieved by the autopsy results?"

Daniela's eyes darkened. "Of course. Who wouldn't be?" She dipped her sugar-covered churro into chocolate syrup and bit into it. Seeing her wrap her lips around the chocolate aroused him. He forced himself to focus on his interview.

"What was your father like?"

She hesitated, her eyes looking downcast, as if remembering. "He was very warm and approachable after he stopped drinking, but before that, well … not so much."

"How long had it been since he stopped drinking?"

She shrugged. "From memory, it was a few years, but it was hard. We started out as quite poor, but when my father got a new job after he stopped drinking we managed to do well. He had lost so many jobs before that …" She paused, raising a hand. "Is this off the record?"

"Of course. Go on."

"He assaulted his boss after he got drunk during his lunch break, then another time, he swore at a co-worker. Both times, he got the sack. Being in and out of work was crazy because my mum didn't earn much as a factory worker. At least now she's retired and will get something from my dad as they never divorced. They were still married."

"Do you know why he left? Did you get a note or an explanation?"

"No, nothing. One day he was with us and then that night he wasn't. But now that I look back on it, he was extra warm and fuzzy with us the day he left, and he must've said 'I love you' so many times. It was like he was saying goodbye, but I don't know what made him leave. He seemed happy with us."

"Hmm. It is strange."

Daniela gazed closely at him. "You mentioned a source that gave you those financial details. Do you know who it is?"

He frowned. "I thought I was doing the interview." He continued, "I don't know, but his information was backed up by the employer and by my own research. It could be someone working for the company, but no one's come forward. Unless your father did private work we don't know about."

"Who knows? He's been a mystery for so long. I'd like to move on and keep the good memories alive."

Her phone buzzed. "It could be important." As she checked the display, her face paled.

His chest constricted. "What's wrong?"

Daniela put her phone in her bag. "Nothing important." She breathed fast and downed the rest of her hot chocolate. "Is that the end of the interview? I need to get going." She jumped out of her seat and rose.

"Of course. There's more than enough here. I'll get this done soon and let you read it before it's published." Daniela showed him to the door, avoiding his eyes.

What had scared her?

Chapter 14

SURPRISE VISIT

A day after the interview, Daniela returned home from a workout at the gym, still wearing track pants and a figure-hugging crop top. She remembered the text message she'd received last night: *Don't you love games?* It had made her toss and turn in bed, thinking about her stalker. Who was it? And would they ever stop?

As she unlocked her front door, she heard a car door slam and loud footsteps approaching. A prickle of fear ran down her spine. Was it the person harassing her with crossword puzzles? Why didn't she carry a weapon? She had her key so she could jam it into his eyes. Slowly, she turned around, gripping the keys tightly. Her heart raced and her body shook, but she was ready.

Daniela swung her right arm, but someone clutched it. "Rafael? What are you doing here? You scared me." She ignored the heat in her loins and the way his lips looked in the night.

He smirked. "I'm sorry, but I had to stop you before you took my eye out." He sighed. "I wanted to show you a rough draft of the article before it's published tomorrow night."

Daniela nodded, opening the door. "You could have emailed it to me. You didn't need to come all this way." Although her spirits lifted whenever he was around.

"Face to face is always better. I can get your immediate response and make the changes quicker this way."

They settled on the couch side by side as he pulled out the draft from his briefcase. Their hands brushed as he handed it to her, and she felt a bolt of electricity in her chest. Even his strong cologne endeared him to her. He wasn't the arrogant man she thought he was. He might have a heart, as well.

She read the article, surprised by its depth in showcasing her life's work. It even mentioned her dance background and ankle injury. The article mentioned her time with her father and his absence from her life. It wasn't exactly an emotional piece, but it did promote her school and reputation, as if there were no other school to match her students. "It's great. Thank you." She lifted her shoulders. "Perhaps take this bit out about my father being out of work and the poverty-stricken bit."

"Not a problem. I'm glad you like it. When I submit it to the editor, we'll add the photos and testimonials. Then hopefully you'll be able to get new students to replace the ones you lost. Not to mention expand into other areas of Spain. Quite the feat."

Daniela nodded. "We shall see, won't we?" Aware of his proximity, she stood quickly. "Care for a coffee or a strong drink?"

"A coffee would be nice."

Daniela headed to the kitchen and put on the kettle. Reaching for the mugs, she turned briefly and noticed his gaze on her. Blushing, she pulled down her top and set the mugs on the counter, then added a container of sugar and a jug of milk to her tray.

She set the tray in front of him. "Help yourself to milk and sugar." She grabbed her own and took a sip. "Tell me about yourself. What made you become a reporter?"

He tilted his head. "I guess I like to be noticed and have a voice, and that's what reporting gives me. I also love analysing and writing without getting emotions involved. It's therapeutic, too."

"So did you not have a voice before?"

He chuckled. "Getting a bit deep, aren't we? Why don't you tell me why you became so enamoured with ballet dancing and teaching?"

Daniela realised she'd got too close and personal and didn't blame him for avoiding the question. "So now I need to answer such a deep question? But then again, I kind of answered it in the interview."

"Not really. But humour me. You can make it as superficial as you can."

Daniela breathed in and out and placed a hand on her heart. "I love getting lost in the dance where nothing can hurt you. The freedom to be in control and the escape as I get to dance through my pain. There's nothing else like it. I love seeing the bright faces of students when they've mastered a dance move. The hugs with their families who share in their joy. Fathers who are proud of their daughters and cannot stop wrapping their arms around their children. It is priceless and worth so much. That adoration."

His eyes held something in them. Sadness, trauma? "I am sorry that your father never got to do that with you, Daniela. Is your father another reason you became a dancer?"

Daniela froze, averting her eyes. "Excuse me a minute." She jumped up and went down the narrow corridor to the bathroom. How could that one statement about her father bring up so much of the past? The way her father verbally abused them. The way he beat her mother and hurt Eva.

Looking in the bathroom mirror at her bloodshot, tired eyes, Daniela splashed cold water over her face and wiped it. Taking a deep breath, she walked back to the living room and put on a cheerful expression. She had to mask her pain.

Rafael leaned forward. "Is everything okay?" She nodded and sat beside him again. "I enjoyed watching you teach. You have a real talent for it."

She grinned. "Thank you, and you have a talent for writing. I appreciate you doing this for me. After what happened with my father, some parents no longer trusted me."

He finished his coffee. Their eyes locked. "Well, it's their loss, Daniela. Just believe in what you're doing and more students will come." He rose from his seat. "Have you heard from Blanca?"

She nodded. "Yes, she's loving Valencia, and said she enjoys that kind of work. But she doesn't want to do it often. I'm sure she and Carlos plan to marry soon."

"Hmm. They do seem to truly love each other. It's very rare to get that kind of love, if at all."

Daniela avoided his eyes and felt something close to disappointment. Was that the way he truly saw love? "We can both agree on that."

"Thanks for the coffee and the chat. Check the newspaper tomorrow. Good luck with your business," Rafael said.

"Of course." She walked him to the door and watched as he stepped into his car and drove off. The house seemed empty all of a sudden.

Chapter 15

A MEMORY

Daniela turned the pages of *La Verdadera Noticia* until she found Rafael's article about her dance school. It had been laid out as a full-page feature, with a photo of two of her students in mid-air, followed by their testimonials of how Daniela challenged them towards personal and professional growth. The article went on to describe Daniela's dance career, the history of the school, her teaching methods, and how she had been devastated by her father's unexpected death after not seeing him for six years. This led to her remembering again how he'd abused her earlier and had neglected her afterwards.

Ruminating about her father, she flashed back to a memory. She was ten years old.

Daniela sat by the living room coffee table, writing in her notebook. Eva sat close by, watching TV while her mother stirred a pot of boiling soup. Her father walked into the kitchen, drunk. Her mother looked up. "Abel, I tried ringing you. Where were you?"

"That's my damn business, Adriana. Now, why isn't my dinner ready?"

She turned off the gas. "It is ready now, Abel. Let's sit. Children, come."

Her father peered at Eva's school report card on the kitchen table. She hadn't done well in most of her subjects. He slurred, "What is this? Why is Eva not doing well in school?"

Her mother stopped ladling the soup into a bowl, her eyes dark. "The teacher rang me and said she will need to do extra classes. She hasn't been feeling well lately."

He turned to Eva, who seemed to shrink as she reached the table. "Extra classes, ha?"

"I'll do better, Papa," said Eva.

"This is not acceptable." He glared, his hands clenching. He grabbed the collar of Eva's shirt and threw her against the fridge. She ran into her bedroom, but he held something in his hand. "That bitch! She can't just run off. I was talking to her."

Daniela stepped forward. "Papa, no!"

Her mother screamed, "Abel, please. She will do better."

Shoving her mother away, he shook his head and staggered towards the bedroom. Daniela ran after him, but he got to Eva before she could stop him. A shattering sound stopped her in her tracks. She swallowed, opened the door and screamed at what she saw.

Eva lay on the floor. Shards of glass were scattered around her face, and blood seeped out of her eye. Her father stood still for a moment, then stormed off, slamming the door behind him.

Daniela shivered at the memory. Why did she even go there when it would do no good? Taking a deep breath, she tried to shake out those bad memories. But it was her father's fault that Eva had only one good eye. It was his fault that she had to endure such trauma, and have nightmares for years. The counselling helped but he'd given Daniela a huge internal scar that would last for the rest of her life.

Making herself a cup of tea, she sipped and focused on the article again. Retrieving her phone from the kitchen counter, she rang Rafael. "Hi, it's Daniela."

"Hello there. I didn't expect to hear from you."

"I wanted to thank you again for the article. It should help the business." She paced up and down the living room floor, wondering what he was doing.

"You're welcome. I had an interesting and cooperative subject, and I enjoyed writing it. So, what are you up to tonight?"

"Not much. I'm having a cup of tea. What about you?"

"I'm making a few notes for an article I'm writing about a series of robberies. I've done one but I'm working on a follow-up story."

"Blanca called again and says hello," said Daniela.

"I imagine you miss not having her around. I worked as a foreign correspondent a few times, but it can be risky work if you get into the crosshairs of people who don't want you writing their business."

"Where have you travelled?"

"I've been to Africa, South America, and different parts of Spain. But the work helps you to become resilient and develop as a journalist. I wouldn't trade the experience for anything else."

"Blanca would have told you that she worked in Brazil for six months, and that the experience wasn't so great. The story she was working on involved a lot of corruption and death in the favelas. It's probably something to steer clear from because you don't know if you're safe writing about that topic."

"Blanca mentioned a bit about her time there. I admire her for going through that kind of trauma. It stays with you even if you move forward. It becomes a part of you and shapes who you are in the present."

"It sounds like you're talking from experience, Rafael."

"Anyway, what else are you planning to do tonight? Anything interesting?"

Having changed the subject, Daniela wondered what demons he had in his closet. She appreciated that they barely knew each other so wouldn't push. "I'm addicted to a Spanish telenovela which airs tonight, so I'll be watching that."

"I prefer documentaries and action stories."

"I do too, but soap operas give me that escape I sometimes need."

"And what would you need to escape from?"

She swallowed. "Oh, life in general. It doesn't always go the way we want it to, but telenovelas can be the spice of life."

"I can understand that, but we make our own choices. Sometimes we have more control than we think, Daniela."

"We have the illusion of control." She didn't want to get into a debate with him and realised she didn't want to send him any wrong messages here. "I'd better go."

"Oh, yes. The famous telenovela. I'll let you get to it. Have a good night."

"You, too." She ended the call, finding that her heart was racing and her throat was dry. She took a sip of the remaining, lukewarm tea and sat on the couch to watch her show. This was definitely an escape from memories she'd rather forget.

Chapter 16

DANCE INVITATION

On a Saturday night, Rafael stood in a queue outside a night club with Carlos, Blanca and her friend, Kim. He'd been invited to Daniela's dance performance at this amazing-looking club in Plaza Mayor. The queue looked a mile long. It was obviously a popular club, yet he'd never attended.

He turned to Carlos who stared straight ahead, looking bored. "What's the story here with Daniela? I know she mentioned doing these dance performances, but does she do them often?"

Carlos shook his head. "It's only occasional. Apparently, an old friend asked her."

Blanca added, "Her friend had some kind of family emergency and asked if she could fill in. It could have been your promotional piece on her that made her old friend think of her, too. It's not only brought her a few new enrolments, but she's had a lot of enquiries which are likely to lead to more business. You've made her famous."

Rafael's heart warmed, a sense of pride in compensating for that first article he wrote about her family. "I'm glad to be of service, Blanca."

Kim beamed. "I like your work, Rafael." He smiled back. "How long have you worked with Blanca?"

"It's been about six months, so not that long. I worked with other newspapers before that, and did some work overseas, too." The queue started moving, but they were still far from the entrance. He revelled in the sounds of giggles between Blanca and Kim as they whispered about something. What he'd give to know what they were amused about. Kim seemed to have a big heart, similar to Blanca, but she also had a quiet confidence and wisdom about her, as if nothing could challenge her. Having a yoga and meditation practice seemed to suit her. "I hope Daniela's okay with me coming with you guys at the last minute."

Carlos slapped him on the back. "You're a friend of ours, and despite not knowing you that long, we sort of like you, Rafael. I'm sure Daniela won't mind. She's grateful to all you've done for her." He turned to Blanca when they moved a few steps ahead in line, not yet close to the entrance. "Are you okay, honey?"

"I'm just thinking about whether we'll get into the club this century," Blanca answered. "We still have a way to go."

Kim chuckled. "It is a popular place, but we need to have patience. Believe me, it is worth the wait. Take this as an opportunity to be in the moment."

"I will hold you to that, Kim. It sounds very Zen, which I would expect from you," Blanca said as she pressed her lips together.

A few more steps and half an hour later, they finally got in. Rafael's eyes bulged at the triangular etchings in the ceilings, the three levels of seating, and the circle of balconies. The shiny dance floor faced the stage, where a Latin trio played. Patrons clapped and bobbed their heads to the music.

When the song ended, Rafael turned to Kim. "This is an exciting place. I wish I'd come here before."

Kim clapped hard over her head. "It certainly is. You should come here with Daniela one night." She winked then turned to the stage. "Daniela is coming on now."

Rafael watched the stage, his heart accelerating at the thought of seeing Daniela. He imagined how her body would look in her dance attire and how the grace of her moves would show the smooth length of her neck.

When the dancers came on stage, he felt a prickle behind his neck and turned. Someone on the balcony was watching him. Rafael craned his neck for a better view, but whoever was watching him had vanished. He thought it was a man in a long jacket and dark glasses. But anyone could be watching anyone in this place. Why was he being paranoid? Rafael looked back up at the balcony again, but the person he'd seen had disappeared.

Daniela pounced onto stage, wearing a tight black and gold-sequined costume. It hugged her body nicely, drawing his eyes to her like a magnet.

She somersaulted and flipped without her hands touching the floor. Amazing!

"What a talent," said Carlos.

Without taking his eyes off her grace and flexibility, Rafael nodded. "She sure is." He couldn't stop staring at her quiet grace. Her figure-hugging clothes accentuated her sexy physique. Other dancers wearing the same costume filled the stage, moving with the Latin rhythms. Daniela twirled and cartwheeled, swaying in every direction. Her passion had him immersed. He glimpsed her joy and pain through the dance. Mesmerised, he did not notice the back of his neck sweating until the tingly sensation found its way down his back.

Finishing, Daniela and the other dancers bowed to the audience and retreated backstage. Rafael wanted to see more of her.

Chapter 17

A NIGHT OUT

After Daniela's dance performance, the group stood outside and waited for her in the warm, breezy air. When Daniela rushed out, she stopped in her tracks at the sight of Rafael.

Blanca and Kim rushed forward and wrapped their arms around her. "You were amazing," said Blanca. She looked over at Rafael with a questioning look. Was Blanca trying to get Rafael's approval of her dance, or trying to match-make them?

"Truly spectacular," said Kim.

They walked towards Rafael and Carlos, with Daniela nodding in his direction, shock evident in her eyes. She hadn't known he was coming, and his chest tightened at the idea that she didn't want him here. He should have turned down the invitation, but Carlos had invited him, and he didn't want to be rude. It wasn't like he had to see her, but he never turned down an invitation to go out.

Carlos approached and kissed her on the cheek. "You need to do that more often. Was your ankle okay?"

"It got a bit sore, but I trained well for it. One dance isn't going to kill me. I mean, it's not like I can do that often."

"I enjoyed it," said Rafael. That sounded bland, even to him.

Daniela averted her eyes. "Thank you." She squared her shoulders. "It's a surprise to see you here, Rafael."

Carlos intervened. "I hope you don't mind, but I invited him at the last minute."

"Okay," Daniela said.

They walked to a nearby bar. The sign over the door showed a painting of a plate, jug, and glasses, and the word "*champinon*." A delightful odour wafted out of a narrow doorway as they walked up the few steps inside.

They made their way towards the sound of Gloria Estefan's ballad, *Con los Anos Que Me Quedan*, one of Rafael's favourite songs. The scents of fried peppers, garlic, and lemon permeated the bar's dark ambience. Crowds surrounded small tables.

Rafael and Daniela found seats on opposite sides of a table. The others sat around them. "I love the smells in here," said Rafael.

A burly waiter approached. "What can I get you?"

Carlos ordered shared meals. "We'll have the grilled chorizo and garlic stuffed mushrooms, the croquettes, your fried squid, fried green peppers, and some bread." They each ordered regional wines and beers. Another of Gloria Estefan's songs came on, *No Sera Facil*.

Rafael and Daniela's eyes locked as they took in the lyrics of the song. He focused on her luscious red lips and beautifully shaped face. Her glossy hair fell in loose strands around her cheeks. His heart yearned to reach out to her as the others spoke amongst themselves. He was oblivious to anyone else. He saw her dainty hands clenched, her eyes shift among the others, and occasionally dart towards him. He had to stop fantasising about what her lips would taste like or how it would feel to brush his hands through her hair. Even the way her body would fit snugly with his.

Carlos nudged him. "Hey man. I was asking if you've been here before."

Rafael shifted his eyes to Carlos. "Oh, of course. A few times with Fernando and a couple of other friends. Love the mushrooms here."

"I haven't been here before," said Daniela. "But at least they have great taste in music. I love Gloria Estefan. She's one of my favourite singers."

Rafael nodded. "I agree. Gloria Estefan is one of the most popular here." He couldn't shake this unusual feeling he was having, and he didn't like it. He had to be on his guard and realise that having emotions and getting attached to anyone was a waste of energy. He didn't need the pain. Rafael had his career to think of. A beautiful woman would distract him from achieving more awards and great stories.

When their food arrived, he delved into a bit of everything. He relished the soft texture and tangy, garlic flavour of the mushrooms.

He ignored the buzzing of his phone in his pocket, but it wouldn't stop buzzing. Blanca eyed him curiously. "You're a popular guy."

"Sorry. I'll put it on silent." Checking the display, he saw five text messages. Should he check them or not? No, that would be rude. He placed it on silent and put the phone back in his pocket.

Blanca looked at him strangely. "Not another message, is it, Rafael?"

Daniela watched her friend. "What message?"

Rafael swallowed. "Nothing, Daniela. All good."

Blanca turned to Carlos, who nodded as if they were agreeing on something. "Rafael, I need to say something. Strange things have been happening to Daniela, and you've been getting these messages, too."

He looked at Daniela, who stared into her plate. "What strange things have been happening?"

"Daniela's had someone play pranks on her. One night they moved our potted plant in front of our home and buried a puzzle deep inside it, but no actual message. Another time, she found a crossword puzzle inside the passenger seat of her car, but she doesn't remember putting it there."

Daniela's face reddened and she touched the base of her throat. "Blanca, please. Don't make a huge deal of it. It's a joke, by someone who knows about my dad and me liking crossword puzzles."

Rafael's lights came on. Was the same person targeting him and Daniela, given it was all related to her father? "What else has been happening to you, Daniela?"

She leaned forward. "I've had a couple of silent phone calls. A text message. Breathing on the other end. Like I said; a joker with nothing better to do."

Kim put down her wine glass. "I hope you are right, Daniela. But it sounds like you might need to report this to the police. What has happened to you, Rafael?"

He took a breath, a part of him not wanting to worry Daniela. "It's nothing. Don't worry about it."

Daniela sighed. "I need to know what's happening, Rafael. If I shared, then you should share. I'm a big girl, don't worry. I can take it. I've been through worse, I'm sure, so spill."

Rafael believed she'd been through worse with her father, and if they pooled their resources, they could find out if something more was going on. "I keep getting these emails about every article I've written about your father. My own judge and jury."

"You need to be more specific," said Daniela.

Rafael explained the emails he'd been getting and the documents he'd received about her father's embezzlement. He also told her about the note he'd found on his windscreen outside the gym. "These sound related, Daniela. Maybe it's the same person who hates your father."

Carlos wiped his mouth, flicking his hair out of his eye. "Check your phone. It might be the same guy with his obsession over Abel."

Rafael nodded and took out his phone. His body turned numb as he read the five text messages. "The same three words have been repeated, saying, 'Fuck Your Article.'"

Blanca clasped her hands together, staring at Carlos in concern. She looked at Daniela, then at Rafael. "But your latest article is about Daniela, not her father. What does that even mean?"

"It means they don't like my latest article, but why?" Rafael faced Daniela. "They're targeting you and your father. Do you have any idea who this could be?"

Daniela turned away, gulping her wine like it was water. She put up her hand to a waiter who approached. "I need another one. Anyone else?" They all shook their heads, and the waiter left.

"What was your written message, Daniela?"

Daniela shivered. "The crossword puzzle said, 'Let The Games Begin' and the text message said, 'Don't you love games?'"

Oh, Christ! He didn't want to think of the worst, but now the heat had been turned up, and they needed to report this to the police. It was no time to leave it alone when it was beginning to feel like they were both being stalked.

Chapter 18

INCIDENT REPORT

The old building of the Policia Local or Madrid Police Station stood out in the busy street, accentuated by its sign and the police car stationed in front. Daniela heaved as she stepped inside with Rafael. The smells of sweat and aftershave permeated the cramped room. A crying child ran rampant, and a policeman raised his voice at a citizen. The queue in front of the desk led almost out the door.

Daniela turned to Rafael with a shake of her head, her shoulders deflating and her mood dim. Was this even worth it when the line was this long?

Rafael exhaled. "This is crazy long."

Daniela nodded. "I know. Maybe we should go." She was thankful it was Sunday, the day after they'd gone out as a group, and didn't need to work tonight.

He shook his head. "Let's give it some time. It might go quickly."

Daniela played with the tips of her fingers. "I hope you're right, but it looks like we have not only locals, but tourists here today. Sometimes even filing out a *denuncia* can take a while." She shifted her feet.

He leaned forward. "These threats are strange, Daniela. Are you sure you don't know of anyone who could be doing this to you?"

She shrugged. "I don't know, Rafael, but I hope it is just a prank. Otherwise, they might escalate in stalking situations like this. I hope the police take it seriously."

Daniela gripped the envelope in her hand. It contained the crossword puzzle and a print-out of Rafael's email messages. "You'll need to show them your phone with those text messages. They might be able to trace them."

The line moved an inch. Blanca counted the number of people in front of her; twenty-five. She realised this was not going to happen today.

An hour later, she knew she was right. The line had barely moved. She'd probably report her case and then the police would forget all about it. "Let's go. This is ridiculous. I can report the harassment online or by telephone. The only problem is that the face-to-face reporting takes priority, but it doesn't matter. This won't get done today, and I need to get out of here. I'm feeling stifled, just thinking about this."

Rafael squeezed her shoulder. "I know it's hard, but we're reporting this. It's too important. We need to show them our phones and report this in case it is something."

Daniela huffed, knowing he was right. If they didn't report it and something did happen, they wouldn't be protected. "Fine then."

Another hour passed before they reached the front. A beast of a police officer took up a lot of space at the counter, but his blue eyes were friendly. "Can I help you, Miss?"

Daniela moved in closer. "I'd like to report a harassment case. I have evidence here in this envelope and on our phones."

He nodded. "And do you believe that this is someone you know?"

Daniela looked at Rafael briefly. "No, I don't know who it is. But it's also been happening to my friend, here."

The policeman checked the email print-outs and the words, *Let The Games Begin,* circled across the crossword puzzle." He leaned forward, clasping his hands. "Any known enemies or conflict with someone you know?"

"No, not that I know of," said Daniela. Rafael explained his situation.

"And how long has this been happening? Over what time period?"

"It started a few weeks ago after my father died, and it was made public." Daniela gave the details of the infamous Abel Lopez. "I've had one text message and two silent phone calls, too."

"Okay, show me your phones." Daniela and Rafael handed him their phones. "I will take a screenshot of these phone messages and attach the digital version to your report file." He gave them each a form. "I need you to both fill these out while I secure these print copies." He handled both phones while they filled out the forms.

A few minutes later, they handed back the report to the officer. "Do you know the reason for this harassment? Why you're both being targeted? No relationship disputes or lawsuit issues?"

"No, none at all, Officer," said Rafael. "This started for me with information I received from a source for an article I eventually wrote. I'm a journalist." He explained the events since he received the first message.

The officer nodded. "I'll get forensics to look over this evidence for any prints. But make sure you keep a journal of dates if this continues." He squared his shoulders. "We'll send this report to the judicial authority, and from there a determination will be made on whether these reported events constitute a serious enough crime under Spanish law. You have not been physically harmed, and with little information to go on, nothing may come of this. You need to be prepared. A number of criminal cases will take precedence over your case." He turned to Rafael. "Can you forward the emails you've received so our cyber-stalking team can look into it?"

Rafael clenched his hands. "Of course."

The phone on the officer's desk rang. "Excuse me a moment." He picked it up and briefly replied to what sounded like an enquiry. When he hung up, he turned back to them. "I'll forward your case to a detective to investigate, and we'll let you know if anything comes of this. In the meantime, if you receive further messages, write them down. Keep a record of everything. If things escalate, call us straight away."

Daniela smiled "Thank you." She walked to the exit, Rafael's hand on the small of her back.

As she was about to enter her parked car, she had the sense that she was being watched. She thought she saw something move behind a tree, but she couldn't be sure. Was her insecurity over the messages making her see things?

Rafael sat in the passenger seat. "Are you okay?"

Daniela became aware of how close he'd moved. She tried to ignore the flutter in her stomach.

She had to focus, and not be distracted by the cute dimples on his cheek or his dark, soulful eyes. Even the way his lips parted as if he wanted to say more. "I'll be fine. At least we reported this."

He gave her a reassuring smile. "I want you to be careful, Daniela. Don't take any unnecessary risks. If you need to go anywhere at night, you shouldn't go alone. I ... just be careful." Their eyes met and lingered there, but Daniela broke the gaze and stared out the window before starting the car.

Chapter 19

GAMES PEOPLE PLAY

Daniela was on her own after dropping Rafael at home that night; Blanca was with Carlos again. Rafael might have offered to visit her at home if he knew she was home alone, but she didn't want him to think she was weak and couldn't look after herself.

Instead, she preferred to enjoy another of her favourite telenovelas with a long glass of wine. She pulled left-over gazpacho and a *tortilla espanola* from the fridge, and set them on the table with her first, healthy glass of wine. She needed it tonight.

She'd had enough of Rafael, needing to get her bearings and bring her emotions under control. She wasn't in the headspace to get close to a man whose eyes bore into her soul, and whose hands she yearned to touch. Men always left her anyway, so she was better off alone.

Sitting at the table, she slurped the soup, then took a bite of a small piece of her omelette. She heard a noise at the front door. Was it footsteps? Had Rafael decided to visit? No, it was too soon.

She swallowed her food, washed it down with more wine, then approached the door. She went back to the kitchen to fetch a knife and gripped it tight. Her breathing accelerated and chills ran over her shoulders as she sidled towards the door, ready for anything.

Daniela opened the door a little, but no one was there. A package lay in front of the door. She hesitated. It was Sunday, and the post didn't deliver on weekends. This package had been hand-delivered. She hadn't ordered anything, and Blanca would have told her if she was waiting on a package—but surely not on a weekend. What could it be?

She picked it up and closed the door, weighing her options. No, the best thing to do was to open it when she wasn't alone. But then again, it looked like a book, and nothing dangerous. It wasn't ticking when she put her ear against it.

Her phone buzzed. The display read, "Save your sister. Pick up the package." Her heart raced and she felt numb for a moment. No, this had to be a joke. Her sister was fine.

She called her sister, but got voicemail. She called her mother, but there was no response there, either. She waited a few minutes, then called Eva again, but still there was no response. Her mother still didn't answer. She thought of calling their friends but didn't know their phone numbers.

Without waiting another second, she ripped the package open. Inside were two books of crossword puzzles, with bookmarks in their pages. One of the marked puzzles was titled "Eva's Challenge." The other crossword puzzle was titled "The Final Challenge."

As her body shook, she closed her eyes. *You can do this. You can do this. Save your sister.* Even if this was a joke, she had to do this just in case. She had to take on the challenge if this was the same person harassing her.

Hands sweating and throat dry, she blinked a few times and focused on the first crossword puzzle. Two separate spaces were highlighted. The clue for number 1 across read "Cross and quarrelsome." She thought of words like *argumentative* or *crabby*. No, these were either too short or too long. She had it. *Contentious* fit, so she jotted the word down. The clue for 1 Down was also highlighted:

"PM in the heart of Madrid." Easy! She wrote *Plaza Mayor* in the spaces. Now, what? What did she do now?

Grabbing her keys and handbag, she rushed out of the door on the assumption her sister was at Plaza Mayor. From her car, she dialled Eva's number, but again it went to voicemail. She called again, with the same result. Oh, God! If something happened to Eva, she didn't know what she'd do.

Daniela sped all the way to the centre of Madrid, leaning forward in her seat, tailgating slower drivers, and cursing behind trucks. Her hands became clammy and slipped on the steering wheel. Her lips and chin trembled. She didn't know how to breathe as she zigzagged through traffic while her leg muscles tightened. She looked ahead without really seeing anything. Her sister's sweet face was in the forefront of her mind, and she struggled to hold back a scream. Blinking rapidly, she fought back dizziness as she wove through the cars, and prayed her sister was alive and well. Whoever was doing this was surely only joking. But she had to take this seriously. She couldn't bet on her sister's life.

When Daniela finally arrived near the Plaza Mayor, she parked the car, not caring that she'd get a fine, and ran with all her strength for eight minutes. She finally entered the public space and passed the horseman statue, the well-kept green lawn, the eateries covered by white umbrellas, and the crowds sitting on the grass. She ran across the concrete ground, manoeuvring through the crowds, wanting to drown out the loud voices and the footsteps, as her eyes scanned like a madwoman's in search of her sister. Surely, she was enjoying her time here and wasn't in any trouble. Maybe her stalker knew she often visited the area and hadn't hurt her. He may have seen her here and stolen her phone.

People stared at her as she squinted in the fading sunlight and squeezed between children, couples and families. Her heart felt like it was exploding out of her chest, and she wiped away tears with the back of her hand. After wandering for at least half an hour, Daniela stopped an elderly woman. "Excuse me. I'm looking for a woman with long, glossy brown hair and blue eyes. Have you seen her?" The lady shook her head. "Wait." Daniela rummaged in her handbag and pulled out a photo of Eva. "This lady. Have you seen her?"

"No, sorry. She is beautiful but I haven't seen the lady."

"Okay, thank you."

Daniela asked a few more people if they'd seen Eva, but no one had. What more could she do? Where the hell was she?

Stepping into a quiet corner of a restaurant, she retrieved her phone and called her sister three more times. Nothing but voicemail. *Damn. Where are you, Eva? Please tell me where you are.*

A boy of about twelve years of age approached and handed her a note. "Wait! Who are you?" Before she could get an answer, he ran off like a speeding train.

Daniela opened the note to read *Fuencarral Street. Find a red motorbike.* Scurrying back to her car, she reached it in fifteen minutes and drove along the street. She was close to a trendy area called Chueca. What was this person doing to her? She was on a wild goose chase when she believed her sister to be at Plaza Mayor.

Parking her car in the street, she wandered through the shopping district, searching for a red motorbike. Passing shoppers, she panted, sweating and thirsty. She felt light-headed. Ten minutes went by before she found the motorbike with a note dangling behind the front tyre. *One word for a type of beverage and an inland terminal that makes connections. Await further instructions.*

Gasping for breath, she made her way back to the car and closed her eyes to interpret the clue. Her body shook as she focused and delved deep inside herself, hoping to God her sister was okay. She didn't know how much more she could take.

Chapter 20

LUCKY ESCAPE

Daniela clicked her fingers when the answer flashed into her mind. *Port* was a type of beverage and a docking place for ships. But Madrid was inland; it had no port. Could the clue mean Madrid's so-called "dry port"? Did that mean that Eva was at the intermodal terminal? It had to be, and Daniela hoped to God she was right because she couldn't think of anything else.

The dry port in Coslada was a half-hour drive through traffic, and Daniela's back tensed all the way. This had to be where he had her, but where exactly would that be?

When she stopped as close as she could get to the dry port, she exited her car and looked around the rows of warehouses, the lines of railway cars stacked with metal containers lined, the forklifts transferring those huge containers onto trucks, and the workers shouting instructions. She smelled diesel, mould, smoke, and gas emissions. The clank and rattle of trucks carrying their shipments echoed along the brick-lined streets. Overwhelmed with the hubbub of activity, she threaded her hands through her hair with her head bowed down. *Where are you, Eva?*

Her phone buzzed with another notification. Chest tightening, she read the new cryptic clue. *Drive one hundred kilometres towards*

Rascafria. New clue: What am I? I am unloved and standing solitary
with a foul smell.

She gasped. Why did she have to drive one hundred kilometres
north of Madrid to a place she'd visited once with Blanca? Why such
a distance? This guy was sending her on wild goose chases, playing
games from one end of Spain to another. But what choice did she
have?

Accepting it, and thinking about her dear sister, she followed the
directions, her hands sweaty on the steering wheel as she headed
towards the quiet neighbourhood. She pondered the clue: what was
unloved, solitary, and smelly? It took her a few minutes to think of an
abandoned building. Was that where her sister was? But why would
the person make her drive to the port on a wild goose chase? Was it
the thrill of seeing her in panic mode?

Over an hour later, she reached Rascafria, but where was this
building? She parked by the kerb, and ran into a restaurant. An
elderly man looked up and smiled. "I'm looking for any abandoned
buildings in the area?" He stared in silence. "Please, I'm on a scavenger
hunt as part of a game and need to know about any abandoned
buildings."

He nodded. "Ha, yes. That makes sense." He put a finger to his
temple while a line formed behind her. "I don't know, lady."

"Thank you." Her body shivered as she made it back to her car,
thinking. She pulled out her phone and typed "abandoned buildings,
Rascafria in Spain." She found a couple, entered an address into her
GPS, and drove. This was madness. How long would she need to
drive for?

In better times, she would have enjoyed the greenery and the
Lozoya riverside, maybe have taken a walk, or even gone for a swim.
She would have appreciated the mountains, the ski resorts, and a walk

along the riverside, but she had a mission to save her sister before it was too late.

She wondered briefly whether she was losing her mind, which would mean that all this was for nothing.

She honked her horn at a truck going slower than she wanted to go. He wouldn't move over to the right lane, so she honked again. When the truck finally shifted over, she pressed her foot down and crossed over two more lanes to get ahead of traffic.

When she finally reached the destination according to the GPS, she found a dilapidated building with two broken front windows in Rascafria. She jumped out of her car and scurried to a ratty wooden door that was cracked around the edges. The door was padlocked, so she picked up a rock and banged on it a few times. The lock wouldn't break. *No!* She spotted a larger rock, hefted it, smashed it with all her might against the padlock, panting as it fell to pieces on the ground.

As she stepped inside, the pungent smell made her feel sick. She peered around the large, open space. Cobwebs filled every corner of the warehouse. Empty boxes and crates lined one entire wall, and a large steel shelf covered the other.

She scurried past the shelving. This could be a trap to lock her inside, but she had to take the risk. As she passed a stack of boxes beside a large steel shelf, she heard whimpers from the back of the warehouse. She ran for dear life towards the sound.

One look at her sister made her cry and almost pass out.

Eva's cheeks were cut and bruised, her lips were swollen and dry, and grazing surrounded her eye. Her hands were bound behind her back. She lifted her drooping head to Daniela. "Help me, Dani...ela."

Daniela held back tears as she wrapped her arms around her tightly, then rushed to untie her sister. "I'm here, Eva. I'm here," she said, stroking Eva's face. "You're safe now."

Eva nodded. Realising she could barely stand, Daniela helped her up, and put one arm around her back. Slowly they made their way outside and into the car, then drove to the nearest hospital in silence. Eva closed her eyes and slept all the way.

Daniela held Eva's hand in the hospital ward, shaking her head and pushing back her tears as she roused from sleep. "How are you feeling?"

Eva sat up, her bottom lip trembling. "Better, thanks to you."

"Do you remember what happened?"

Eva shook her head, her hand trembling. "I don't remember much of anything, Dani."

Bile rose to her throat at the fragile state of her sister. "What do you remember?"

Eva turned her head towards the window, taking deep breaths. She swallowed. "One minute I was at the supermarket, then the next minute I'm in that warehouse. How did you even know I was there?"

Daniela didn't want to worry her further. "I have to call Mum and let her know where you are."

Eva pressed her lips together and faced her again. "I told her I was visiting my friend after the supermarket, so she wouldn't be worrying right now." Hugging the blankets, she asked, "Are you going to call the police?"

Daniela nodded. "I'll be right back." She walked outside.

She had to call the police about this. Whoever had sent her those messages had done this to Eva. But first, Daniela needed to call her mother. She found a table in a nearby tea room and pulled out her phone. Checking the display, she saw she'd missed a number of text messages, repeating the same message: *Call the police and she will die next time.*

As her breathing accelerated, she bowed her head into her hands and wondered what she would do. She couldn't gamble with her sister's life. This seemed to be an act of hate, but who hated her, and since when did she have an enemy? In her mind, she hadn't wronged anyone, and had always lived an ethical life. Sure, she'd been a party girl, and enjoyed nightclubs, parties, and dancing, but she'd never hurt anyone in her life. It couldn't be any of her ex-boyfriends, particularly her last one, who had wanted to end the relationship. It wasn't possible. But who?

Placing a call to her mother, she held her breath. "Mum, it's Daniela. Listen, Eva's in hospital, but she's all right."

"The hospital? What are you talking about, Daniela?"

"I'll explain when you get here, Mum. She's at the San Carlos Hospital. See you soon." Now she had to come up with a lie about how she had found her sister. She didn't want to take any risks, so the lie would have to be convincing. For all she knew, this madman was bluffing about killing her sister. But she wouldn't take that chance, not when he'd beaten her so badly. Now, all she had to do was convince Eva to not contact the police.

Chapter 21

A SWEET KISS

The next Tuesday evening, Rafael rang Daniela's doorbell. He hadn't seen her for several days, and when he'd called twice, he left messages, but she hadn't called him back. He hadn't seen or heard from her since Sunday afternoon, and a part of him shivered at the thought that something was wrong.

Blanca answered the door. She looked at him quizzically and ushered him to the living room. Daniela sat on the couch, scrolling on her phone.

"Like I said at the office, she's been acting strangely," Blanca whispered. "You might be able to get her to open up."

His chest constricted as he nodded. "I will give it a shot. Thanks, Blanca."

"I'll leave you guys to it. I'll be in my room if you need anything." As she walked down the corridor, she looked back over her shoulder with a dark look in her eyes. Had she been spooked by the stalker, Rafael wondered? Did something more happen?

He sat beside Daniela, who responded by scooting to the other end of the couch. "Hi, Daniela. "Are you okay? I tried calling, but you never called back."

She tilted her head. "I've been busy. I didn't think I had to report to you, too."

Her eyes masked pain, and her fingers trembled. "I called you twice and you didn't return my calls."

Daniela got up and paced the floor with her hands on her hips. She sighed and peered at the ground. "Like I said, I've been busy with work. Sorry."

He looked up. "After what we talked about and reporting things to the police, I was worried. I hadn't heard from you. Did something happen?"

Daniela pursed her lips and sat back down, a little closer to him. Her floral scent and direct gaze drew him closer. She moved back, as if she had mixed feelings about their proximity. "I'm sure Blanca would've mentioned I was staying with my family for a couple of days."

"And you couldn't take a minute to return my call?"

Daniela scoffed. "You knew where I was, so you didn't need to worry. You're not my keeper and I don't owe you anything, Rafael. So don't act like you're my babysitter."

He ignored her fury. "With everything that's happened, I was worried when you didn't return my calls."

Daniela's eyes darkened. "Can you just let this go, Rafael? I am tired and don't need this right now. If you need your ego stroked, go find a woman to love in one of those brothels. I don't need this right now."

"That's a low blow, Daniela. I can get any woman I want in a bar. I don't need to go to a brothel. That's not my scene, and never was."

Daniela shook her head, her eyes squinting. "Wow! You really are a pompous ass who thinks he's God's gift to women. No doubt you volunteered to write that article just to stroke your ego, not to help my business. Your motive is ambition and greed, and that's all this arrangement was. I wonder if you've ever helped anyone in your life."

Rafael's hands clenched. He hated how she was partly right. Their arrangement—if that's what it was—was more than just promoting his own ambitions. He'd genuinely wanted to help her, and cared for her in ways he didn't want to. He wasn't a monster who didn't have feelings, and he didn't want her getting hurt. Right now, she was lashing out at him to cover something up, and he was determined to find out what it was. "You don't know anything about me, really, Daniela. You are making assumptions based on what I choose to share with you, and I don't have to share anything with you. But we need to work together on this. We don't know who's sending these messages. Tell me what's going on."

"Nothing is going on. I wanted to spend time with my family. Is that a crime?"

"No, it's not. But when Blanca tells me that you've been checking your phone multiple times, and sleeping with a baseball bat under your bed, I worry. Show me your phone? Where is it?"

Daniela shrugged. "I am not saying, and you have no right to invade my personal business. Can you just leave?"

"It is my business when a stalker's going after both of us. Now show me the damn phone or I swear I'll—"

Daniela leaned within inches of his face. "You'll what?"

"I will force it off you. Now give it to me, Daniela." He saw it on the side of the couch and reached behind her for it, but she grabbed it first. "I know something's on that phone. Hand it over."

Daniela frowned and put up her hand. "This is bordering on harassment and bullying. Stop this, Rafael. Please."

He sat stock-still, their eyes locking, lingering, bodies close. If he moved his head an inch, his lips could touch hers. If he lifted his hand, his fingers could trail the outline of her mouth and caress her flushed cheek. A brush against her thigh aroused him as he lifted his hand to stroke her right cheek. She closed her eyes, seeming to enjoy his touch. When she opened them, he shifted, inched closer and closed the gap between them. His lips brushed against hers, his tongue circling her mouth to taste mint and spices. Reaching around her waist, he deepened the kiss. Daniela reciprocated for a minute before she pulled away and stood up.

"I think you should, go." She averted her eyes.

He missed her lips already. "I'm sorry, Daniela, if I crossed the line."

"You did. Now, please go."

Rafael rushed out of the house without looking back. But he could tell that she had enjoyed the kiss as much as he had, and they'd done it under the worst of circumstances.

Chapter 22

INJURY

O n her way to the dance studio on Thursday, Daniela stopped
at her mother's house to check on Eva. On opening the door,
her mother looked at her strangely. "Daniela, darling. This is a
surprise. What brings you by? Don't you have your dance classes?"

"I do, and I won't be staying long, Mum. Is Eva here?"

Eva rushed up to Daniela. "We have stuff to talk about, Mum.
We'll be in my room."

Adriana angled her head and rubbed her hands. "O ... kay."

Daniela followed Eva into her room and shut the door behind her.
"How have you been, girl?"

Eva shook her head as she sat on a chair. Daniela sat close to her, on
the edge of the bed. "I am still a bit rattled, but I'll get there. I still
need to know how you found me, and why you're not calling the
police. What is going on? We don't know who we are dealing with
here, Dani. I sure as hell don't know why I was kidnapped, or who it
was."

Daniela took a breath, staring at her shaking hands. A chill
permeated her aching shoulders and neck. If she told her sister the
truth, it would put her in more danger. It was best if she didn't know
anything. "Are you sure you don't remember anything? A smell, a
voice. Anything?"

Eva crossed her legs and rubbed her chin. "No, I don't remember anything, Dani. I'm pretty sure I didn't see the guy. He must have drugged me, then somehow got me out of that supermarket and into his car. I didn't like lying to Mum when you told her I got mugged in the street." She frowned. "I'll ask you again, Dani. How did you find me? Did the kidnapper ask for money?" Daniela shook her head. "You have to tell me what's going on here. We've never had secrets from each other. Never. So don't start now. I can take whatever you tell me." Her eyes hardened. "If you do not tell me how you found out, I will spill everything to Mum. You know I will. She thinks you've been in touch with the police, but you still haven't, have you?"

Daniela knew that her sister wouldn't let up, so she relented. "No, Eva. He threatened your life if I call the police. Please understand that I am doing this to protect you."

Eva's eyes widened. "Who the hell is this guy, and why is he doing this to us?"

Daniela shook her head. "I don't know. There's something you need to know, but promise you won't tell Mum anything yet. I need to figure this out on my own for now."

"I promise, Dani. How is this related to you? To me?"

Daniela explained the stalking incidents, the text messages, cryptic clues, and crossword puzzles. "Please don't say anything. I don't want Mum to worry. As long as you're safe, that's the main thing."

"But who could this be, Dani? Someone you know, an ex-boyfriend?"

"I don't know, but I'm going to figure it out without the police. I have no choice."

Eva pursed her lips. "What about that reporter, Rafael? Wouldn't he be good at investigating these sorts of things? Maybe he can help."

Daniela's throat dried up. "That pompous jerk! He just wants a bigger story, and I don't trust that he won't write about this. If anything, it's safer if he doesn't know."

Eva fixed her eyes on her. "Why are you blushing, Dani?"

Daniela fidgeted and ran her fingers along the quilt cover. "What?"

Eva's eyes lightened, as if she needed respite from their morbid discussion. "Oh, you like him, don't you? Admit it."

Daniela sighed. "Of course not. Like I said, he's a jerk."

"Hmm. Whatever you say." She walked to the window and drew the blinds, then turned back to Daniela. "I keep checking and rechecking my surroundings, and I am getting tired of watching my back. When will this stop?"

Daniela took her sister's hands in her own. "Now you listen to me. He will not hurt you as long as I don't tell the police. I think he likes the thrill of scaring us, that's all. I don't think it will escalate." She was lying to herself. Her intuition told her the situation would likely get worse, but she didn't want to scare Eva.

"Do you remember the time Dad tried to scare us?" Eva asked. "He was so drunk, he picked up the knife in the kitchen and threatened to use it if we didn't have his dinner ready on time."

Daniela's chest heaved. "I remember. It was scary. Also that time he threw me across the coffee table, and I had to get stitches across my forehead. But it was the worst with your eye. I wish I could have stopped him. I tried, but I wasn't fast enough."

Eva wrapped her arms around her. "Oh, stop it! He was horrible when he drank, and kind when he didn't. Then when he got help and stopped drinking, he was even better. And I wish I knew why he left us, but we'll never know. He's dead, and we'll never get the chance to learn why he left, Dani."

"I know, but we can hold on to the good memories, Eva." She pulled away from her sister and opened the door. "I have to go. Will you be all right?"

Eva nodded. "Of course. I'll be fine, but I am thinking of self-defence classes. Please keep me in the loop, Dani, and if there is anything I can do, let me know."

"Great idea, sis. I'll be fine." She rushed out of the room, gave her mother a quick kiss on the cheek, and left.

"Okay, ladies. Remember to keep practising for the upcoming competitions. Memorize the routine and make sure, Catalina, that you buy new shoes. Those ones are worn out."

Daniela watched the girls rush out of the room into the waiting arms of their parents. Walking into her office, she stopped short at the sight of Sofia crying near her desk.

Touching her on the shoulder, she asked, "What's wrong?"

Sofia wiped her nose with a tissue, lifted her shoulders, and looked past her. "I just broke up with my boyfriend, but I will be fine, Daniela. I'm sorry."

"No, I'm sorry. Is there anything I can do?"

Sofia cleared her throat and looked behind her. "Hi, Diego. She turned back to Daniela. "Listen, let's grab a late dinner. Diego wanted to take me out, but I need a friend to come with me, too." She faced Diego. "Is that okay?"

He beamed. "Of course, it's okay. The more the merrier. I have to make the most of Madrid before I go back to Barcelona."

"When are you going back?" asked Daniela.

"In a few weeks. The company wants me to set up new projects, so it will take a bit more time. I am thoroughly enjoying this city. Now, how about tapas for dinner?"

"Sounds great," said Daniela.

Daniela finished locking up and turned to face Sofia and Diego. A noise in the distance alerted her to attention. Damn motorbikes! Always breaking her eardrums. She took a breath and moved ahead of Sofia and Diego across the road. They followed her behind when the loud rumbling noise came closer. Finally, a motorcycle drove past them, the driver in a helmet and dark glasses staring at her. Why was he staring?

When she reached the other side of the road and turned along the footpath, the motorbike rider made an abrupt change. He slowed down and turned, riding up the footpath towards Daniela.

Diego yelled, "Daniela, watch out! Daniela!" Before she was able to register what was happening and move out of the way, Diego ran headlong in front of her and shoved her out of the rider's path. The motorcyclist knocked Diego to the ground and sped off. Daniela's legs froze and her heart raced. Taking calming breaths, she turned to see Sofia kneel by Diego's side.

Daniela rushed to Diego's side. His arms were grazed and bruised, and he rubbed his leg. He moaned and closed his eyes briefly. "Are you okay? Do you need a doctor?" Daniela babbled.

Diego slowly opened his eyes. "I'll be fine. I think it's only a sprained ankle. Did you see the bastard?" Sofia helped him up slowly on unsteady legs.

"I didn't get a look at his face because of his helmet and dark glasses." Daniela helped him to a nearby bench and sat beside him. "Thank you, Diego for saving me. I didn't know what was happening, and you jumped ahead and risked your life for me."

Diego shook his head. "It's fine. I will be fine. Are you girls okay?"

Sofia nodded. "I'm good."

Daniela added, "I'm fine too, but you need to take a breath and rest for a minute." She wondered if her stalker just tried to run her down.

"We should call the police," said Sofia.

Diego shook his head. "No point. We didn't see the guy's face, so it'll be a waste of time. It's not like the police will view this as a priority case."

"Maybe you're right," said Sofia.

Diego rose, limping towards the restaurant. Sofia put her arm around him. "Why don't we take a rain check on that dinner?" he said. "I am in so much pain right now."

"You should see a doctor," said Daniela. "Or I could take you to the hospital."

"Nothing that a good rest won't fix. I will be fine, Daniela. It will heal in a few days, I'm sure. You have a good night." Daniela watched them walk towards Sofia's car, wondering what just happened.

Chapter 23

AN INTERVIEW

R afael drove at a leisurely pace through the picturesque Salamanca neighbourhood in north-east Madrid. Fernando had assigned him to interview a young woman named Teresa. She had submitted her brief story to the newspaper, keen to help other women who had survived domestic violence.

He followed the GPS tracker, taking in the sandstone buildings, parks, and greenery. He passed the art museum and Salamanca University. It was a scenic place he'd never visited, even though this area certainly had a strong aesthetic appeal for tourists.

When he arrived and parked by the kerb, his eyes widened at seeing the large property. It was one of those designer apartments he loved, and it was not for the poor. Colossal trees, shrubbery, and wide-open space surrounded the home with an air of calm, instantly feeling as if terror had not occurred in this house over a year ago.

Rafael clutched his black leather satchel, his palms sweaty on the handle as he made his way up a long, winding path to the apartment. He hadn't interviewed for a human-interest story in a while, having concentrated on crimes and general news. But something about this story appealed to him.

A cute little brown-haired girl with chubby cheeks opened the door, then stood cross-armed and wide-eyed. The little girl's feet shuffled. "Is your Mummy home?" he asked. Instead of responding, the girl rushed off, and her mother walked to the door.

"I'm sorry. She gets shy." Teresa smiled and drew a quivering hand across her blonde fringe. The sunlight glossed her shoulder-length hair, and her bright green eyes bore into him as if wondering whether to trust him. She had experienced a world of pain, yet resilience remained. "I'm Teresa, and you must be Rafael from *La Verdadera Noticia.*"

He nodded and held out a firm hand. "Yes. It's great to meet you."

The woman had a quiet grace. "Do come in."

The contemporary apartment had a large entrance hall with a gas fireplace. The living area had high ceilings and large windows, allowing natural light to stream in from an open atrium. Teresa led Rafael to the terrace, then sat on a cushioned cast-iron seat. A tall cast-iron bookshelf stood inside the door, a chaotic pile of documents on top of books about trauma and domestic violence.

Teresa gave Rafael a questioning look. The poor woman said nothing as Rafael sat opposite her.

"I admire your courage to tell your story. I really appreciate you coming forward," Rafael began. "I know it can't be easy for you."

Teresa was quiet for a few moments, her eyes peering into the distance. "It's okay. I want my story to go public. I need to help other women experiencing domestic violence." She rose. "Can I get you something to drink?"

Rafael's heart warmed at her candour. "No, I'm fine. Thank you."

"I'll just get my daughter busy. She loves the *Toy Story* movies." She rushed away from the terrace.

His eyes roamed. He thought about how cosy, yet modern her home was. Her brief had described how her husband had almost killed her one night when her daughter was at her grandmother's house. He knew all too well how hard it would be for the daughter to lose a parent.

When Teresa returned with a half-smile, Rafael took out his recording device. "Is it okay if I record the interview? It's purely for my own notes, and it'll be erased once I've written the story."

"That's fine." Teresa sat, crossed her legs, and took a deep breath as if preparing for a torture session. She'd be reviewing her pain, but she held her posture straight and waited for his questions.

"I'd like to start off by hearing a bit about your life growing up with your parents and siblings. Your childhood experience."

She nodded. "Okay. Nice and easy to start with. Thank you."

Rafael smiled and pressed the record button. Teresa recounted her life story with a strong tone, and light in her eyes. The love she shared with her family growing up must have given her the strength to endure the violence to come. "And how did you meet your husband?"

Teresa swallowed. "At a work function, where he said all the right things, and gave way too much detail about himself. It was as if he needed to convince himself of his lies. He was a real charmer and knew how to win me over. Once we got married, Javier changed dramatically. He wanted to control the way I cleaned the house, the way I cooked, the way I dressed, and even the way I hosted dinner with his friends. I could never do anything right, and whenever I argued, he'd hit me. It started with slaps, and then escalated to punches, then a kick in the gut, then a combination of everything. He broke my teeth and fractured my collar bone once, but I had to lie and tell everyone that I fell in the backyard. I couldn't go to work for weeks. On one particular night, he almost killed me, but the telephone rang and jolted him out of his rage. It gave me a chance to hit him back and run for my life. A kind old man found me unconscious in the street and called the ambulance. He saved me that night."

Rafael's chest tightened. He didn't know what to say to ease the trauma. "I am so sorry, Teresa. I cannot even imagine what you went through." He squared his shoulders. "And how are you coping with life now? Without having to look over your shoulder, thinking your husband is out there watching your every move?"

Teresa took a calming breath. "I'm coping well now. As you know, it's been over a year since I reported him and kicked him out, but I still have nightmares. They are occurring less and less frequently." She looked haggard. "Domestic violence creates a living hell. You stop breathing, always having to be cautious with the way you do things. I tried to think of ways to please him one hundred times a day. I never knew if I'd earn a punch or a slap or a long beating. It depended on his mood, which kept fluctuating."

Teresa went on, describing more incidents with her husband, and her daughter's birth. "Javier became worse when she was born. I had less time for him. When my daughter, Tia, was asleep, the nights got worse. I didn't know what would happen." She swallowed and wiped away a tear. "A few times he raped me. Poor Tia woke up one night and found me bleeding in the bathroom. No young girl should have to see her mother in pain like that. I hope she'll forget that in time."

A torrent of tears streamed down her face. "It was the not knowing that was the worst. Constantly walking on eggshells and wondering if today was the day he would rape me again, or if he would beat me senseless, or kill me. Or was it the day he'd go after my family? Other times, he would be all sweet and kind and buy me roses out of guilt." Rafael's spine went cold as he clenched his fists. "My daughter was the best thing that came out of a terrorising situation. And I am blessed to have her. But she will never get to know her father."

"Did Javier ever seek out custody of Tia?"

She placed a hand over her heart. "Thank God for small mercies. No, he didn't much like children, and he never wanted Tia. He had ignored her since birth."

Poor Teresa had suffered, but at least Javier didn't want to see his daughter. She was better off without a man as cruel as him for a father.

Chapter 24

OFF THE RECORD

While waiting for Teresa to return from the kitchen with hot chocolate, Rafael looked around the terrace, his eyes wandering over the bookshelf with its pile of documents laid on top of a multitude of books. He spotted a bank notice threatening foreclosure on her apartment. From what Teresa had explained, her loser husband had been wealthy, so why was the apartment not paid for? Had he spent his money recklessly and left her with debts? Was it to pay her back for leaving him? He didn't want to pry, but it broke his heart to know that after enduring domestic violence, she was being pressured by a bank with the threat of homelessness. Once he'd published her story, he could set up a fundraiser for Teresa for help from empathetic readers and fans. How would he broach the subject delicately?

Teresa's face was pale when she returned. She set down a tray of mugs of hot chocolate and *mantecados*, small shortbread cookies that he loved. His mother had made them when he was a child in their better days.

Rafael sat back down. "I'm sorry. I didn't mean to pry."

"It's okay. It'll probably be public knowledge if I lose this beautiful house, but maybe it's a blessing in disguise. There are too many memories here."

Rafael picked up his mug and took a sip while Teresa did the same. "I understand, but if you want to talk, I can listen."

Teresa knit her brows then sighed. "I want this to be off the record, and don't want it to be published in any way. Please promise me that."

Rafael nodded. "Of course."

"My husband, Javier was unfaithful in our marriage. But during that time, I noticed small amounts of money being deposited into our account. I didn't think anything of it and thought he might have gotten a raise at work in his IT business. I questioned him and he mentioned investing in shares and making a good return."

Rafael nodded. "That makes sense."

Teresa shook her head. "That's what I initially thought." She frowned. "I contacted the company he invested in, but they didn't have his records, and said that he didn't have shares in the business. He lied to me."

"Did you find out where the money came from?"

"Once he left, he took all that money with him and closed our joint account."

This poor woman, who had not only suffered physically and emotionally, but financially, too. "How much money did you lose, Teresa?"

A stream of tears fell down her cheek. "It wasn't only Javier's savings, but mine, too. I worked hard to save that money." She closed her eyes as if praying. "I lost over two hundred thousand Euros, and now I am struggling to pay the mortgage on only one wage."

The room suddenly seemed colder. "Let me help you, Teresa. I can organise a fundraiser, explaining that you were cheated by your husband."

Teresa lifted her head, her hands clasping her mug. "I appreciate the help, but I'm going to sell the house. The bank's been great with allowing lower monthly payments, but they can only hold on for so long. It's a blessing in disguise. That man destroyed my life in this house. He was not only physically, emotionally, and financially abusive, but manipulative as well. He lied about many things, but was such a charmer in the beginning. I believed his lies. I have to leave this place. Too many bad memories."

Rafael drew his cold hand through his hair. "You've been through a lot." He handed Teresa his business card. "Keep the card handy, and please let me know how you're going. If you change your mind, give me a call. I'd be happy to help."

"Thank you. I appreciate you keeping this financial issue to yourself. I look forward to the interview being published in your newspaper."

Rafael rose. "I'll make this story count." He smiled and leaned forward to shake Teresa's hand. "Take care of yourself. A photographer by the name of Marco wasn't able to come today, but he'd like to take pictures of you and your daughter in your home. Is tomorrow morning at nine o'clock okay?"

"Yes, that should be fine. And remember to emphasise that I'd like to be a voice for all abused women." Teresa walked him to the door.

"Where is Javier now?"

Teresa frowned. "I have no idea, but he mentioned leaving the country. The police stopped monitoring him after he left me."

On the drive back to the newsroom, Rafael's head weighed heavily on his shoulders, and goosebumps covered his skin in spite of the day's warmth. He couldn't believe the damage this man had caused. He hoped Teresa could let go of the past and move forward to a bright future with her daughter.

Chapter 25

A FIRE

That evening, Rafael lay on his couch with a bottle of beer in his hand. A sense of helplessness washed over him as he thought of Teresa. The poor woman was still being punished after Javier's departure, so it was a blessing that the man was out of the country. A man who not only violated and cheated on his wife, but had made her destitute, too.

As he switched channels, the doorbell rang. It was Fernando with a dozen beers. "I bring liquid gold, Rafael."

Rafael swung open the door and ushered his friend inside. "No need, man. I have the same stuff in my fridge. As my boss, you shouldn't be getting me drunk."

Fernando opened the fridge and swung the beers inside. "As your friend, and not your boss tonight, we are putting aside our problems and letting go." He helped himself to one of the beers and threw the cap inside the sink.

Rafael moved over to the couch. "I wonder if you ever spend time with your wife and kids. Doesn't she ever complain about you being here so often? Not that I'm complaining."

Fernando joined him on the couch, and placed his right leg over the left while sipping his drink. "Space is what we need right now." He looked away, darkness filling his eyes.

Rafael put his beer on the coffee table. "What's going on? Are you and Rosalia having problems?"

He nodded. "I'm thinking of moving out, Raf. We both need time out. I feel like she hates me at the moment. Even the kids seem to be better off without me. I miss so much of their lives, but that's on me. I sometimes put work first, but I have responsibilities."

"But you can't move out. You need to work it out together and communicate. Your kids need a father. Don't be absent in their lives. I know how hard it is, man."

Fernando fixed his gaze on his friend with a questioning look. "Listen, I appreciate your candour, but don't make this about you. All kids are different, and I'm different."

Rafael pushed back images of his father's frail hand. "I'm not making it about me. I'm talking about keeping your family together for you and your children. You're a great guy. Let them get to know you."

Fernando took a sip of his beer and wiped his mouth with the back of his hand. "I know you grew up without a father most of your life, but it's not the same thing. He died, and your mother struggled to cope. Two different situations here."

"I know, but you need to be there for the kids. Don't make this about them when it's about you and Rosalia."

Fernando nodded. "I'll be there for them, but for now we need time out. I'm moving out by the end of the week."

Rafael knit his brows. "I am here for you. Any time."

"Thanks, Raf. You're a good friend." He turned to the TV and Rafael flipped to a football game. They watched in silence and sipped their beers. He couldn't believe his friend was separating from his wife. He loved Rosalia. She had a good heart, but she'd obviously had enough of his workaholic ways. No doubt Fernando would need to make sacrifices if he wanted to stay married. Rafael was thankful that he was single and didn't need to worry about a relationship.

Then his mind flashed to Daniela's full lips and the curves of her body. But as much as he was attracted to her, he didn't need to commit. He could fight his yearning, his desire, and his need to keep her close.

Rafael turned back to the TV, a heaviness filling his chest as he thought about his friend, hoping he could work it out. He went to the bathroom, and when he returned, Fernando was on his phone, his face pale and eyes dark.

"Okay, we'll cover the story. I'll give Emilio a call. Thanks." He ended the call and started another. "Hey, Emilio. I need you to cover a story tonight. A fire at a dance school. I'll text you the location." He nodded, ended the call, and tapped on the screen of his phone.

A fire at a dance school? "What happened?" Rafael asked.

Fernando hesitated. His hands clenched under his chin. "That was my police contact." He averted his eyes. "I know you and Daniela are friends, so I wanted Emilio to cover the story rather than you."

Rafael's heart beat fast and his throat felt dry. "Are you saying that Daniela's school is on fire?"

He nodded. "Yes, the firefighters are getting it under control as we speak. Go and be there for her, Raf." He paused. "I'll go home, and get the details about it tomorrow."

Rafael drew back, his breath *whooshing* out of his chest. What the hell! How could this happen? "I'll see if she needs help. Thanks, Fernando."

"Don't mention it, Raf. Be there for her. Support her. I can tell how much you care about her."

Rafael's surroundings felt surreal, dizziness settling in. "I have to go."

Fernando slapped him gently on the shoulder. "I'll see you tomorrow."

After his friend left, Rafael grabbed his car keys and rushed to the garage.

Rafael parked his car as close to the dance school as he could. As he jogged closer, his heart broke at the sight of balls of fire shooting from the building, and the black soot surrounding it. A huddle of people stood near, whispering and shaking their heads while firefighters hosed the blaze. A police car stood by, while a policeman directed passers-by.

As he drew closer, the smoke filled his nostrils. Daniela stood with slouching shoulders, close to Blanca, Sofia, and her cousin, Diego, who were talking to a second policeman.

Emilio walked up. "Hey, Rafael. I spoke to Daniela, and she's devastated, naturally. But I'll do the article justice, man."

"Thanks, Emilio. I appreciate that." He nodded, gave him a reassuring smile, then approached Daniela and the others. "Hi, guys. Daniela, I'm so sorry. What happened?"

Her eyes were raw red and her hands shook. "I can't believe this is happening, Rafael. Who could do this to me? My students were counting on me, and now they've got nowhere to go. Thank God we didn't have classes tonight. Someone could have got seriously hurt, or worse." She bowed her head and put her face into her hands.

He didn't know what to do but admire the way she held herself together. He wanted to reach out to stroke her hair and wipe away her tears, even wrap his arms around her and tell her it would all work out. But he did none of that.

Diego stared at the blaze. "It is such a shame. I've seen the kids and how much they love it here." He stroked Sofia's shoulder as she shook her head, fighting back tears.

"Those poor kids. Where will they go now?" Daniela said.

Blanca replied. "We're here for you, Dani and Sofia. Anything you need."

Sofia cried as she faced Daniela. "We will bounce back, Daniela. We will."

Rafael stood among the others while the firefighters battled the blaze for the next hour. Once it was over, Daniela fell to her knees and cried. Blanca and Sofia put their arms around her and cried, too. Rafael felt helpless as he stared at Diego, thinking he must feel the same.

Chapter 26

DISCLOSURE

After the firefighters left, Rafael followed Daniela and Blanca home. Daniela dropped her phone on the kitchen table and threw herself on the couch. She rested her head back while Blanca and Rafael watched her with concern.

The police had interviewed her briefly, and explained that they might need to follow up, depending on the outcome of the fire investigation. If it was foul play, they would investigate further.

Blanca gave her a reassuring smile. "I'll make us a cup of coffee." She headed into the kitchen while Rafael sat on the armchair beside Daniela. He flung one leg over the other and took a deep breath.

Daniela looked up at him briefly with tired eyes as she rubbed the side of her throbbing head. What was she going to do now? She had let her students down when they had competitions coming up, and nowhere to do their final rehearsals. Perhaps the studio wouldn't take too long to restore—but who was she kidding? The fire had spread throughout most of the building. She didn't have much hope.

When her phone buzzed, her heart leaped. She rose quickly, but Blanca picked it up before she could get to it. Luckily it was password protected. "I'll get that, thanks."

Blanca stared at her strangely. "Sorry." She handed her the phone."

Rafael's shoulders rose. "Are you still getting strange messages?"

Daniela put her phone aside, gripping it tightly in her lap. She had risked her sister's life, and she didn't want to risk anyone else's. The less they knew, the safer they'd be. "Listen, my building was just set on fire and that's all I can focus on right now, Rafael. You don't need to be here. Don't you have an early start for work tomorrow?"

Rafael sighed. "I am here out of concern. If you remember, I wrote an article about your school, and I met some of those students. Don't you think I care?"

Blanca returned with three cups of coffee and set them on the table. "Dani, I'm sure you'll get news about the fire soon."

"I'll have to find another building or the students will miss out," Daniela replied. "Some of them don't have the space at home to rehearse, so it is up to me to find them somewhere to go until I can repair the damage."

"Your sister rang here the other day when she couldn't get hold of you," Blanca went on as if she hadn't heard Daniela. "She was worried about you, and let something slip out."

Daniela's hands shook as she picked up her cup. Had Eva told her something about her kidnapping? "What do you mean?"

"She mentioned being in a hospital. Why didn't you tell me, and how did it happen? Eva wouldn't tell me anything."

Daniela crossed her arms. "Nothing you need to worry about, Blanca." She yawned. "I'm tired. I'm going to bed." She avoided their eyes, realising that they suspected she was holding out on them.

Rafael paced the carpet, his hands in his pockets. "What are you not telling us, Daniela?"

She shrugged. "I won't risk anyone else's life. This is my problem to fix. Let it go."

Rafael stepped close to the couch, leaning over Daniela. "Please tell us the truth. I thought we were working as a team on this, and if something happened to Eva, we need to know. Remember, I can help, and do my own investigating. We have to work together or you're risking your own life. It's my job to find things out, so use me as an asset. This person is hurting me, too. Don't you see? This affects both of us. My anonymous source has something to do with your father, which means that this person could be your stalker. Someone is angry about something, and we need to find out what that is."

Daniela's stomach churned and her throat clammed up. Christ! What if she was putting Rafael in more danger by keeping quiet? Could they work together without involving the police? The stalker warned her against contacting the police. But Rafael was not the police. Could they work as a team to find him before he did more damage, especially if he was the one who set her building on fire? But she couldn't be sure. As far as she knew, it could have been an accident. Until the firefighters investigated, she had no way of knowing whether the fire was intentional or accidental. "Fine. Drink up as it's going to be a long night."

Rafael's face paled as she recounted Eva's kidnapping and the clues she'd received. "Dear God! Why would they kidnap your sister? Is it about hurting you, or is this about your family?"

Blanca moved closer to her friend, and put her arm around the small of her back. "Oh, Dani. I am so sorry you had to go through that. Why didn't you tell me? I could have been here for you. I could have helped to find her."

"You were away in Barcelona, and there was no time, girl. This was more about keeping me on edge. I don't think he wanted to hurt Eva, but probably needed to scare me into submission. It's as if he wants to get me riled up, for whatever warped reason. And he obviously enjoys crossword puzzles like me."

Rafael's body stiffened. "Your father had a crossword puzzle by his bedside, Daniela. You don't think ..."

Daniela sighed. "The autopsy ruled he had a heart attack. No foul play."

Blanca's shoulders rose. "There are medications that can make things appear that way, so who really knows? But we cannot jump to conclusions here. We need more evidence. It's too early to say that his death was suspicious."

Daniela turned to her. "We? You are not involving yourself in this, Blanca. I am not risking anyone else's life. This seems to be about Rafael and me. I don't know why he's targeting us, but we need to find out."

Rafael gently squeezed her shoulder, his face softening, and his eyes warm. "If you can't go to the police, then we'll do our own investigating, Daniela. We can pool our resources. We won't let this bastard win. You've got my full support."

"I might not have a job for a while, Rafael, but you do. I can do this on my own."

He got up from the armchair, finished up the remainder of his coffee, and leaned in. "I will make the time after work hours and on weekends. We can go out tomorrow night and discuss things. Sleep on it, and I'll talk to you tomorrow."

Her heart warmed, and she yearned to wrap her arms around him. She wanted security, and the reassurance that things would work out. Rafael made her feel safe and warm. He made her feel other things too, but she had to focus on their mission. "Fine, Rafael." She showed him to the door. Their eyes locked.

He gave her a reassuring smile. "Have a good night. Bye, guys."

Once Rafael left, Blanca hugged Daniela tightly. "I didn't want you to go through what I went through last year, Dani. I never wanted this for you. But whatever I can do— research, a shoulder to cry on, you name it. If I can reduce the pressure on you, tell me how."

Daniela patted her back. "You went through far worse than I am, Blanca. And I love you for being there, but for now, Rafael and I will do our research." She refused to think her stalker would escalate, but she would be ready for him.

Chapter 27

A SHADOW

Rafael sat in the staffroom the following day, engrossed in casual conversation with Blanca and Emilio when Fernando entered, biting into a chorizo-and-cheese roll. "Hey, boss. What's up?"

"How are you doing with Teresa's human-interest article? The deadline's today, and we need to get the online version done."

"It's ready, Nando. I only need to double-check it. Once that's done, I'll send it over to you."

Fernando took the last bite of his roll, speaking with a mouthful. "Great, man. I'm sure you've done it justice." He walked out of the staffroom, wiping his mouth with the back of his hand.

Emilio leaned forward, toying with his hair. He forked his cheese omelette from inside a plastic container. "I don't know if you wanted to check the article about that fire at the dance school. I managed to get a few quotes from parents and students. Then I'll do a follow-up article once we know the cause of the fire. The firefighters mentioned it'd take about a week to investigate. But it could have been worse."

Rafael clenched his hands, bile rising in his throat. "Don't you dare down-play that fire, Emilio. Daniela's lost her livelihood and now she has no place for her students. It was a big enough fire, okay? Big enough to leave her students stranded. Who knows how long it'll take to get it all repaired."

Emilio put up his hands. "Hey, man. I didn't mean it that way. Jesus! Get a grip." He shook his head and shovelled more egg into his mouth.

Blanca moved closer in her chair. "Don't blame Emilio, Raf. He's just giving you the facts. It was a bad enough fire, but it could have destroyed the whole building. At least it is repairable, and I'm sure Daniela will find another venue."

Rafael fixed his gaze back on Emilio. "I'm sorry. I didn't mean to bite your head off. I just have a lot on my mind, and you were in the firing line. Are we still friends?"

Emilio slapped Rafael's hand. "No worries, dude. I won't take it personally, and we are still friends. I'll give you the article to check later this afternoon. I want to make sure it's sensitive, seeing as you know Daniela better than I do."

Rafael nodded. "Thanks, Emilio. I appreciate you thinking about that."

Emilio closed his container. "I'd better get back to it. See you guys later."

Blanca smiled at Emilio, and waited for him to leave before she focused on Rafael, who was finishing his lunch. "What is really going on with you, Raf? I've never known you to take a story so personally. Do you have feelings for Daniela?"

His face reddened as he averted his eyes. "That's ridiculous. She's a friend and we're both being harassed by some psycho. We have to help each other out. I'm worried."

Blanca knit her brows. "It's natural for you to feel worried. Are you sure that's all this is? I am sensing something more."

Rafael got up and threw his plastic wrap into the bin. "I have to get back to work." He rushed out before she could respond. He passed the other reporters and editors, all quiet and solemn as they concentrated on their computer screens, researching or writing their latest article.

He thought about Blanca's question. As if he had real feelings for Daniela. It was about survival. They both had a madman stalking them, and they could easily be the same person, given that her father seemed to be at the centre of it all. He needed to research Abel Lopez's history more closely, especially the time after he had left his family six years earlier.

He sat at his desk and put Daniela to the back of his mind. He opened the article about Teresa and scanned for proofreading errors, but could not stop thinking of Daniela; her dark, sad eyes, the tremor in her voice when she had watched her school burn down, and the way she'd looked at him, as if she wanted his support. If only he could have wrapped his arms around her, or comforted her in the way she needed to be comforted. But he couldn't bring himself to do it when others were around.

Rafael rotated his shoulders to get the kink out of them. He clicked the spell check icon and fixed his minor errors. When the article was ready to be sent to the senior editor, he headed to Marco at the photographer's desk. "Have you got those photos of Teresa ready?"

Marco was short and stocky. "Sure do. I've got a few here we can select from. Let me know which ones capture the mood of your article." He opened a series of image files on his screen. One photo showed Teresa smiling in her kitchen with her arms crossed. Another photo showed her with her daughter, Tia, on her lap, sitting in the living room.

"I like these ones." Teresa sat with Tia in a warm embrace, and another photo showed Teresa's softer side inside the terrace. The final photo showed Teresa beaming with pride as she sat in her garden, but Rafael saw another figure in the background.

"What's that in the background? Can you blow it up for me?"

Marco zoomed in. "It looks like someone watching her from behind this fence. It kind of looks creepy. A neighbour perhaps?"

An uneasy sense pricked his shoulders. Rafael wondered if this person looking over the fence was a friendly, but nosey neighbour. "Can you block him out?"

"Sure thing," said Marco. "No dramas."

On his way back to his desk, Rafael passed the conference room, where he saw Fernando having a heated conversation on his phone. His face turned red and he shouted into the phone, but Rafael couldn't make out what it was about. Dismissing it, he returned to his desk and squared his shoulders, hoping Teresa would be proud of the article and photos when they appeared in the next day's edition. He had it ready to send to the editor for final proofing, and then to the web editor who would prepare the online version.

He would check in on Teresa and make sure she was okay. He was curious about her neighbour. Surely he was friendly; not everyone was out to get them. He decided recent events had made him paranoid, but he had to make sure that her neighbour was not bothering Teresa.

When he returned to Teresa's house after work, Rafael wondered whether he should tell her about the neighbour in the photo. The few minutes he waited after ringing the doorbell felt like twenty. He shuffled his feet and put his hands in his pockets. When the door swung open, he freed his hands and smiled.

Teresa angled her head with a questioning look. Tia stood hid behind her, holding onto her legs. "Rafael. What are you doing here? Did we not finish our interview?"

He sighed. "I wanted to show you something in one of the photos we took. See if you can tell me anything about this neighbour. It's good to have people close who look out for you."

She opened the door further and bent down low to speak to her daughter. "You go play with your toys in your room, Sweetie, while Mummy talks to this nice man." The little girl nodded and ran off. Teresa led Rafael into the kitchen, where they sat at opposite sides of the table. "Can I get you a drink?"

He shook his head. "No, thank you. I won't be staying long." He took out his phone and opened the photo he needed. "Is this your neighbour?"

Teresa reached over for her reading glasses on the table and put them on. She picked up the phone and peered at the screen. "I can't be sure. This man's wearing glasses, so I can't see his eyes, but the shape of the face looks familiar." Focused on the screen, she shook her head.

"Are you sure? Could it be your neighbour?"

Her face paled. "He's about eighty years old, and this person's younger. Much younger." She swallowed and continued to stare at the phone.

"Does this neighbour have a son or a friend who might have visited that day?" An icy chill ran down his back. Was she safe staying here?

She shrugged. "As far as I know, he and his wife only have a daughter, but I could ask him if he has a relative, or friend who's younger and might have visited. But they went out tonight, so they're not home now."

"The article will be in the paper tomorrow, Teresa. It will be a testament to your strength and endurance, and a voice for other women. If you need anything, please call me."

"I will, and thank you. I'll speak to my neighbour tomorrow and let you know what he tells me. I'm sure it's a friend or extended family member."

Rafael shook her hand. "I'm sure it is. But we'll block him out in the photo. I'll talk to you soon." As he wandered out of the house, he couldn't help wondering whether someone else was watching her.

THE LOVE OF MY LIFE

Pinned Brad, his hand still in the spa, his wet hair, clinging to his forehead. "I'll talk to you soon." As he watched her behind the bar, he could tell he was going to suffer...while she was watching her.

Chapter 28

DESIRE

D aniela followed Blanca and Kim through a narrow walkway inside a nightclub. After hours of cajoling, she'd relented to having a night off from her business troubles. It had been almost two weeks since the fire, and luckily she'd found a temporary space until her own school was repaired. At least she had insurance.

She clutched her bag strap over her shoulder, and her mind scattered as they passed a sofa lounge until they reached a set of small couches in front of a stage. In the middle of the ceiling hung a silver disco ball. The dim lights cast a blue glow across their faces. A few young couples danced on the large rectangular dance floor to the samba and African-inspired rhythms of a Latin band.

Daniela pressed down on her tight-fitting red dress that showed her trim figure. She sat beside Kim, who wore a long, black slim-line stretch cotton dress with wedged shoes. Blanca wore a wine-coloured strapless dress. She went to the bar and returned with a tray of drinks, including a cocktail for Kim, a sangria for Blanca, and a champagne for Daniela. She leaned forward and dug her teeth into a juicy strawberry placed inside the glass before sipping her drink.

Kim leaned forward. "How is the new building for your school? Is it suitable for the students?"

Daniela thought about all the enquiries she'd made for rental space, and how it had taken her a week to find suitable premises. "The students are happy for now, but I've lost a few more on the way. I don't blame them, Kim. I haven't been reliable lately, and the mess with my father hasn't helped. Then the fire happened. I don't know what's going on. Why did this have to happen? Especially so close to competitions and performances."

Blanca reached out and patted her hand. "It's not your fault that the electrical heater was faulty. It happens, and at least your insurance will pay out."

Kim tilted her head. "Was that heater new?"

Daniela drew a dainty finger through her brown-black hair. "It was, and I complained to the manufacturer about it. They apologised and said they'd look into it, and compensate me. This company has a good reputation, so I don't know what happened." She didn't want to think her stalker had arranged this and made it look like a faulty heater. What evidence did she have? It wasn't like she could prove anything.

Blanca looked at her quizzically. "Have you heard anything more from your stalker?"

Daniela shrugged. "It's been quiet these past two weeks, and I wonder about the fire."

Blanca squinted. "Wonder what?"

Kim shook her head. "Do not even go there, Daniela. The fire was an accident. I am certain that the stalker realises you have a safety network, and can easily go to the police."

Daniela shook her head. "But that's the thing, girl. I can't go to the police because he's threatened me. I have to do my own investigating."

Blanca finished her drink. "Do not do anything stupid. Report everything to the police. Things have been quiet now, but you've got the messages on your phone. I understand you didn't want to risk

Eva's life, but this cannot go on." Her phone buzzed, and checking the display, she beamed. "Oh, Carlos and Rafael are on their way over. They wanted a night out, too."

Daniela grimaced, not wanting to see Rafael when she had problems concerning her feelings around him. She didn't need distractions. "Did you tell them we were here?"

Kim leaned forward, pointing her finger. "I know what you are doing, Daniela." She remained silent. "It is written all over your face that you're attracted to Rafael. You want to fight it but can't. Give in to your feelings. Rafael is a nice guy."

Blanca touched Daniela's shoulder. "From where I'm sitting, I think he has feelings for you, too, Dani. Maybe it's something you should explore."

Daniela drew back. "I am not in the headspace for a relationship, ladies." She counted on her fingers. "One. I have no luck in relationships because men leave you in the end anyway. Two. I have a stalker in my life, and three. I am focused on getting my dance school back on track. Too many reasons why this would never work. Besides, he can have any lady he wants, and I am sure he's just a player in the relationship department."

Blanca shook her head. "That's where you're wrong. I've known him for six months, and he has had a hard life. He didn't get into specifics. But it's a life he now appreciates. At least that's what he told me."

Daniela turned to Kim. "Enough about me. Anyone interesting on the horizon, Kim?"

Kim sighed. "Fine. Turn the tables, Daniela. But in my case, I will probably steer clear of men. None of them have worked so far, and I have given up the search." She shook her head. "My parents expect me to marry a Chinese man. They'll probably try to arrange a marriage soon, given my age."

Blanca sighed. "You're only twenty-six, younger than me by a year."

"You need to stand up for yourself, girl," Daniela said.

"I agree," said Blanca. You're a grown woman, and still young, so there's no rush."

Kim gave them reassuring smiles and put a finger on her temple as if to ward off a headache. She looked out over the swarm of people and remained silent. She'd had a tough time with a gangster boyfriend several years earlier, but at least she had been able to end the relationship.

Once they finished their drinks, Daniela stood. She needed a distraction from thinking about men. "Why don't we dance? I don't get to do enough of it at work."

Blanca fixed her gaze on her friend. "Great idea. Let's put the problems behind us."

Kim rose and pulled Blanca up. "Daniela has prescribed fun, so let's have fun."

Daniela's chest warmed, grateful to have supportive friends who could make her forget her problems for a while. She squeezed between a group of girls swaying to the music, her friends following to a spot near the stage. The music reverberated as she followed the beat and rid her mind of memories and current problems. Tonight was about fun and forgetting about everything, particularly her past. She would live in the present and not even think about Rafael.

Someone brushed behind her, then touched her on the shoulder. With a gasp, she turned to meet Rafael's striking eyes. Her chest tightened at the way his hand lingered on her shoulder. "Rafael. Blanca said you were coming."

"Hi, Daniela. I hope you don't mind us crashing your night out," he shouted in her ear. The back of her neck tingled with sweat.

She shouted over the music. "It's fine, Rafael." She waved to Carlos, who wrapped his arms around Blanca and kissed her hungrily on the lips. Oh, why didn't they get a room?

"Let's dance." Rafael looked her up and down with eager eyes as Kim joined them in the dance. Daniela's throat dried and her gaze kept focusing on Rafael's full lips, and the way his toned, taut body swayed to the Latin rhythms. A part of her wanted to wrap her arms around him, and the strong scent of his cologne drew him towards her like a magnet. No, she had more important things to think about than Rafael.

Chapter 29

A DANCE

Rafael's eyes ran over Daniela's slim figure. Her tight red dress left little to the imagination. He swayed to the music as they intermittently locked eyes. His heart soared at the way she shyly turned away when he noticed her staring, and the way she bit her bottom lip when nervous. He wondered what it would be like to draw his hands through her silky hair, or what it would feel like to tantalise that lower lip she kept biting. *Oh, stop it!* This was getting him nowhere. He had a job to do, and that was to keep them both safe from whomever was harassing them. He had to be smart about this. Daniela was a smart woman who didn't like to be controlled. What she'd been through trying to save her sister from a kidnapping must have been gut-wrenching. This crazy bastard loved playing games to instil fear, but Rafael was up for the challenge.

Daniela whispered to Kim, who walked off the dance floor. She turned to Rafael, leaning in to shout in his ear. He was drawn to her floral scent and full rounded lips, her breath caressing his skin. "I'm taking a break after this song."

Rafael nodded. He watched Carlos and Blanca enveloped in each other's arms as they danced, seemingly oblivious to those around them. One song rolled into two more while Daniela's gaze remained on Rafael. Finally, she touched him on the shoulder. "I'm out."

Rafael held on to the small of her back as Daniela walked to a small couch where Kim sipped from a tall glass. Daniela whispered in her ear and her friend cackled.

Nearing Daniela, he asked, "Would you like a drink?"

"Sure. I'll have a champagne." When she licked her lips, he wondered if she was flirting with him.

Pushing through other patrons to the bar, a man shoved his way through the crowd. Some of the patrons hurled abuse. The man was obviously in a hurry to leave.

At the bar, Rafael shouted, "A champagne and a light beer, thanks."

The towering bartender nodded. He pointed ahead. "That guy that just left wanted me to tell you something. He forced me to write it on a note, too." He handled two glasses while Rafael gazed curiously.

"Do you mean the guy that just shoved his way through just now?"

The bartender nodded. He unfolded a note. "He said 'What begins but has no end and is the ending of all that begins?'"

Rafael didn't want to think about that. "Who the hell was this guy? Did you get a good look at him?"

The bartender shook his head. "He wore a cap and glasses. He was average height, and I could hardly hear him with all the noise."

"Can I keep that note?" He scanned the crowd all around, wondering if the guy had returned.

The bartender handed him the note. "Sorry, man. But he seemed to know you." The bartender placed the drinks on the counter and Rafael tapped his card for payment.

"Anything else you remember?" The bartender shook his head. "Thanks." When he returned to Kim and Daniela, he handed the champagne to Daniela.

A minute later, he jumped at a slap on his back. Christ! Had the guy come back? When he turned, Carlos gave him a strange look. "Sorry, Raf. Didn't mean to scare you. Are you all right?"

"Yep. Can I get you guys a drink?"

Blanca moved over to his side. "I'm good. You can sit here next to Daniela. Carlos and I will get our own drinks. We'll be back later."

As they left, Rafael gripped his glass and sat beside Daniela, who shifted closer to Kim. He scanned the nightclub again, the bass sounds reverberating in his ears. Couples kissed on other couches, and groups stood near the dance floor, gyrating to the music. Others pushed their way through to the bar upstairs, or greeted friends. Why was he even here? He couldn't talk freely with Daniela because of the loud music, but he savoured the vibe and energy of the place.

A distinguished looking man leaned towards Kim. "Would you like to dance?"

She hesitated, then looked over at Daniela, who shrugged. "Sure." She got up and followed the man to the dance floor.

Rafael felt jealous of the glass that Daniela lifted to her lips. She looked at him curiously. "You seem spooked, Rafael. Are you okay?"

He turned to Daniela with a broad grin, not wanting to worry her. Why worry her needlessly when they could enjoy the night? No doubt her friends had brought her here to forget her troubles. But given what they'd been through, he wondered if he could be their stalker. "I'll tell you later. I want to enjoy my drink."

She nodded. "O ... kay." She took another sip and played with her hair. Their thighs brushed together, and as he glanced in her direction, she crossed her legs. The bare thigh made him yearn for her.

A slow dance played. Couples on the dance floor changed positions. He turned to Daniela, who stared straight ahead as if distracted. What he would give to know what she was thinking as she drew a lock away from her eyes. He could see the rapid movements of her chest as if she was breathing heavily. Did she yearn for him as much as he yearned for her? Why over think it when they could get respite from their issues and have fun. "Care to dance, Daniela?"

She shook her head. "I don't think so, but thanks."

He leaned in and shouted in her ear, wanting to stroke her lobe. "Just one more dance. A way to forget your troubles, Daniela. I promise I won't bite."

She hesitated and peered at the couples dancing. "Fine." She got up and followed him onto the dance floor until they found space in a corner. He looked at her awkwardly and pulled her into his arms, holding her by the small of her back. She wrapped her arms around his neck and swayed to the ballad. Her body fit snugly with his as they gazed intermittently into each other's eyes.

Closing his eyes as she looked the other way, he whispered into her ear. "You need to relax. Give yourself permission to enjoy yourself."

"It is a bit hard when a crazy person's after you."

He wanted to reassure her but couldn't. "I'm going to help you catch this guy, but for tonight, let yourself go. Let yourself feel the music." He wanted to get out of there, but he didn't want to make her think he was making a move and spook her. They were only dancing, and it didn't mean anything. Why let this psychopath control their lives and keep them on edge with his stupid riddles and cryptic clues? If only he'd seen the guy who left him that riddle, but he was obviously dealing with someone who enjoyed manipulating others and keeping them on their toes. Maybe he was just a stalker who would eventually get tired of his games. What if he had nothing to do with Daniela's father? But then again, what if he planned to hurt them for his own warped reason? He needed to dig further into Abel's past, but he would have to get Daniela on side first. Do it at her pace.

When they had danced to several slow songs, they headed back to the couch to find it had been taken by another couple groping each other and kissing. Rafael turned to Daniela awkwardly as his eyes roamed, wondering where Blanca and Carlos were. "Would you like another drink?"

Daniela shook her head. "No thanks. I'm leaving soon." She turned away from him. "Oh, Blanca and Carlos are coming this way."

Rafael waited for his friends, and they left the nightclub together. When he touched Daniela gently on the shoulder, she winced, and he wondered if she yearned for him, too, but didn't want to show it.

Chapter 30

A GAME PLAN

D aniela rubbed her sleepy eyes the next day as she opened the front door. She stepped back at seeing Rafael in tight jeans and a white shirt, which fit him like a second skin and showed off his biceps. He had his phone in his hand. She pushed down her need to run her fingers over his tanned skin. "What are you doing here? It's Sunday and I wasn't expecting you."

He stood cross-armed. "Sorry. I didn't mean to wake you, but we need to talk."

She shook her head. "Come in." They went the living room and sat beside each other. Daniela pulled the sash of her dressing gown tighter when Rafael's eyes lingered on her chest. Quickly, he looked away. "Why are you here exactly?"

"Where's Blanca?"

"She spent the night at Carlos's place."

"Can I take you to lunch today? I know a great rooftop bar in the city."

Daniela swallowed. "Is this a date, Rafael?"

He chuckled. "Oh, right. You think I'm asking you on a date, but I'm not. Purely a way to map out a game plan for how to catch this guy. If he doesn't want police involved because of his threats, then we'll be the police."

Daniela hid her disappointment, a part of her wanting it to be a date. "Oh, well, if it's to do that, then fine. I can tolerate lunch with you." She rose.

His eyes lit up. "Great." He put his hands in the pockets of his jeans as he got up too. "Okay, I can wait for you in the kitchen to get ready. Do you mind if I grab a drink?"

"Of course not. I won't be long." She walked towards her bedroom and wondered if he was staring at her from behind. She couldn't stop wondering what it would be like to feel his body against hers or to trail her lips around his neck and shoulder, but she shook away her thoughts and focused on getting ready.

Daniela sat across from Rafael in a light-weight timber chair amid a multitude of tables. The rooftop bar offered a dizzying view of the city's skyline, mountains, and forests in the distance. Christina Aguilera's old ballad, *Pero Me Acuerdo De Ti,* played in the background. Rafael got lost in her eyes as they listened to the lyrics of the song, until a burly waiter broke the quiet to take their order.

Rafael had driven his sporty car to the bar in silence, turning to her repeatedly as if he wanted to say something, but holding back. Obviously, something last night had spooked him, but what was it? Was he in two minds about telling her the truth?

"What's your plan, Rafael?"

"Before we discuss that, I wanted to let you know about last night." He peered into the distance, focusing on groups of people taking their seats opposite them. "I didn't want to say anything or worry you, but it sounds to me as if we need to be on our guard, and get to the truth as soon as we can."

"Okay." She frowned. "What happened last night?"

The waiter brought their drinks and left with a smile. She drank a little, then lay her hands in her lap and pressed her lips together. Her eyes focused on Rafael's lips, and she recalled that one kiss, but they weren't in a relationship. She had to focus.

He sipped his drink then lay it down gently as if he needed time to think. "The bartender gave me a note, but he might be throwing us off. Trying to get us rattled. It might not mean anything."

Daniela tilted her head. "Get to the point. What was in the note?"

"A riddle: 'What begins but has no end and is the ending of all that begins?'"

Daniela's body froze. Her head ached. "Christ!" She stared out over the vista, allowing the breeze to cool her flushed cheeks. It couldn't be, could it? "Death? Is that what he means, Rafael?"

Rafael nodded. "That's the only answer I can come up with, but we could be wrong. Or as I said, he wants us to feel debilitating fear, so he can manipulate and control us. He might escalate, or he might just be playing a sick game."

"Okay, so tell me what we can do," said Daniela. "If this has something to do with my dad, do I need to speak to my mum? She might know something about his enemies."

Rafael nodded. "That's exactly what I was thinking. You do need to talk to your mother about your past. This guy seems to react whenever I write articles about your father, and he's only been on the scene since your father died."

Daniela swallowed, wondering whether her mother would be in the state of mind to talk about her father. But how could she ask questions without telling her what was going on? "I can do that. Perhaps visit her during the week, but I can't tell her what's happening. I don't want to worry her about any of this."

"I agree. At least for now." He looked up as the waiter brought a paella rice dish with muscles, prawns, peas, and calamari for Daniela.

The aroma of seafood made her salivate. The waiter set down another seafood dish for Rafael. *Gambas al ajillo*; prawns in a clay dish in hot olive oil, garlic sauce and chilli, and dropped a basket of crusty bread on the table., The smells of garlic and chilli wafted through the air.

Rafael dipped his bread into the garlic sauce and threw it into his mouth. He looked up. "Let me know what she says, but I think we should start this way, then look at other options if that fails."

"What other options?"

"We can discuss that later, but in the meantime, I'll use my resources to dig into your father's past. I can go back to his workplace and ask more questions, but I want to do it discreetly in case this guy's watching our every move. I can talk to his old friends, too."

"What if this is about you, Rafael, and I'm mixed up in it? I don't know anything about your life. Care to share?"

"No, this is not about me, Daniela. I am sure it has to do with your father. Whatever he got into couldn't have been good. This person might be going after his family because your father scammed them out of money. We don't know why he left you, and what he really did during those six years. What if this is a disgruntled client?"

She shook her head, her chest aching. "I still refuse to believe he embezzled funds. He wasn't the type to scam people. What if he was set up?"

Rafael leaned forward, chewing an oily piece of prawn. "In all fairness, Daniela, you didn't know your father in those last six years. He was violent. Don't forget that. He might have gone back to drinking. He might have got mixed up with the wrong people. We'll get to the bottom of it."

Daniela's hands shook as she put down her fork and looked him straight in the eye. "Do not tarnish my father's name like that. He changed over the years, and he was only violent because of the drink.

It's a disease. You, as a reporter who researches everything, should damn well know that."

His eyes softened. "I'm sorry. That was insensitive, but we need to be prepared for anything. You need to be prepared for the worst, Daniela. It will protect you in the long run."

They finished their food in silence. Daniela realised she might have been too harsh when Rafael was only trying to help. But he was right. What if she didn't know her father as well as she thought she did? What if he had been hiding a secret? She had a right to know why he might have embezzled in the first place. But it didn't make sense when he had a well-paying job.

Daniela broke the silence. "Can we talk about something else? This topic is leaving a bitter taste in my mouth. Why don't we focus on you?" Rafael flinched. "Why don't you tell me about yourself? For instance, why you decided to become a reporter."

He wiped his mouth with a napkin and turned away briefly, and she wondered whether he'd reply. "I always wrote as a young child. It gave me that escape from my problems, and it was my survival when things were at their worst. Later in life, I wanted to give people that same escape, and the inspiration to know that we can all learn by reading about common issues. Reading about relatable stories. It's the best thing in the world to know that I have touched people's hearts and made a difference. People learn from stories."

Daniela finished her paella and put aside her plate. "And here I thought it was only about the money and your unrelenting ambition."

He stared right through her, and her face warmed. "That might be a part of it, but mostly, it's about the issues, and helping people through others' journeys. It's rewarding to get the acknowledgement and recognition for my hard work."

His phone on the table buzzed. He looked up. "Sorry, it might be important." He checked the display, and his mouth turned up at the corners. He sighed with relief, then sipped his wine and lay down his glass.

"Is there a reason for the smile?" Daniela asked, smiling back.

"You have a nice smile," Rafael said instead of answering. He stared into her eyes, but she turned away.

"Can you not change the subject please? If we are working together, I should know everything that happens to you. It could mean something."

"A lady I interviewed was worried about someone watching her when one of our photographers took photos of her. She had a violent ex-husband, and feels a bit paranoid with others. But she spoke to her neighbour, who said that his nephew was staying with him, and that he got curious about the photo shoot."

Daniela's heart became heavy. She knew all too well about violence. "Where's the ex-husband now? Was he arrested?"

"He was, but it didn't stick. Apparently, he had a good lawyer, but he has agreed to stay away."

"Jesus, that's awful. That poor woman and what she must have gone through."

Rafael nodded and reached over for her hand. "I'm sorry. After what you went through, it's probably the last thing you need to hear."

The gentle warmth of his hand brought her not only a sense of comfort, but also arousal. She took a breath and pushed down waves of nausea, thinking about the woman experiencing violence. "It's all good, Rafael. I am a big girl and have bigger fish to fry, so don't stress. But you did a good thing watching out for her."

He leaned forward. "Thanks." Haltingly, he continued. "Let's change the subject and move on to less morbid things. What kind of entertainment are you into?"

Daniela's eyes lit up. "Oh, that's easy. Dance performances. All kinds, and even flamenco shows. I love the sexiness of the dance and the emotions spilling out of their pores. It is so intense."

"Funny you should mention flamenco shows. I came across a flamenco dancer who was friends with your father. I'm meeting with him next week, and hopefully he'll be able to tell me something we don't already know. We might have to get tickets for a flamenco show. I'll let you know if that's the case. If he proves not useful, we can still see a show."

Daniela's chest tightened. Could this be the break they were looking for?

Chapter 31

A BABY PHOTO

Later that day, Daniela sat on her couch, peering at her mother. Adriana blushed. "Why do you need to know about your father? He was a drunk until he got help and stopped drinking. I have no idea what you even mean by the past." She focused on the distance as if she was hiding something.

Daniela decided to give her mother just a little of the truth about Rafael. "Someone's been communicating with Rafael, the reporter who works with Blanca. Someone's been harassing him about Dad and commenting on the things he wrote about him. I'm just wondering if Dad had any enemies when he was living with us."

She shook her head and crossed her arms. "No, never. He got along with everyone, Daniela dear. He had turned his life around. In those last six years, he might have made enemies, I cannot tell you. I never heard from him again."

"Is there something about Dad I should know? Are there any secrets? I get the feeling there's more to Dad than you're letting on. He would have made a lot of enemies when he was drunk. Or maybe he made a wrong decision in business."

Her mother shrugged. "What can I tell you? Nothing that I am aware of." Her breathing accelerated and her eye twitched. She was lying about something.

"Please, Mum. I know you're hiding something from me. What is it? Why did we move away from our original home?"

"Why does anyone move? For a better life and a nicer house." She got up abruptly. "You can wait here for me, but I need a few things for dinner. Will you be staying? Eva will be home soon, and we'd love to have you."

Daniela shook her head. "No, I'll be going shortly, but I'm happy to wait for Eva. You go to the shop." This was her chance to snoop around and find something of value.

After Adriana left, Daniela checked through the window to make sure that her mother had gone. Then she ran to her mother's bedroom and began looking through her closet. All she could see on the upper shelf were boxes of shoes and her father's old socks. Daniela couldn't believe her mother kept some of her father's clothing. She pulled coats off hangers and checked the pockets of all her father's remaining jackets and other clothes that her mother had kept. She found nothing.

She searched under the queen-size bed but found it empty. She opened drawers and a trunk, but all she found were more old clothes, handkerchiefs, blankets, bedsheets, quilt covers, pillowcases, and framed photographs of her father and the family. Where else could documents be? Surely there had to be something related to her father's life.

Of course, the garage! Realising she'd wasted a lot of time in the bedroom, she rushed to the garage which housed her father's old toolbox, empty cardboard boxes, picnic blankets and chairs, and a cupboard filled with her and Eva's old school textbooks and picture books.

As she flipped through a story book she'd read as a child, something fell out from between the pages. Picking it up, she saw it was a photograph of a baby. It was neither she nor Eva, but rather a chubby baby boy wearing a blue singlet and a nappy over his roly-poly legs. A cute boy, but who was he? She'd never seen this picture before. Was he one of her parent's friends' children?

Putting the photograph in her jeans pocket, she flicked through documents inside a plastic box on the bottom shelf of the cupboard. At the bottom, she saw old school reports, more old children's books, and stationery. No doubt her mother hadn't cleaned up this part of the garage in many years. Another photo fell out of the box, this one a young toddler posing with Daniela's parents. They weren't smiling at the camera. Her mother's eyes looked dark with worry, and her father's eyes squinted in anger. This toddler looked like the same boy in the baby photo. He had grown up in this one

With both photos in her pocket, she returned to the living room and waited for her mother. She came up with all kinds of explanations; the baby boy was someone they babysat, or a neighbour's son. It couldn't be that they'd had another child other than her and Eva. Ridiculous to think they'd had another child when this boy could be anyone. Where was her mother? She needed answers.

Another thought came to mind: Did her father leave them for another family? Was this young boy the product of another wife or girlfriend, and he'd left them for his other family? That had to be it. But then again, why was her mother in the photo?

The roar of the engine in the driveway alerted her to her mother's presence twenty minutes later. She gripped the photos tightly. When her mother entered, she held them out.

"Who is this baby, Mum?"

Her mother's face paled, and she dropped the bag of groceries on the ground. "Dear God!" She became flustered.

Daniela helped her return the groceries to the bag. Setting the bags on the table, she asked again. "Who is this young boy, Mum? You have to tell me the truth."

Her mother sighed as she clasped her hands. "I am not having this conversation with you, Daniela. I want you to leave. Please."

Daniela stood up, inches from her. "I have the right to know who this boy is. Did Dad have another family? Is that why he left us all those years ago? For this other son of his? Who's the mother?"

Her mother didn't answer, but rather focused on a spot on the wall as if that would give her a clue as to how to reply. "I can't get into this, Daniela, and I won't."

"It's true, isn't it? My father cheated on you with someone else, and this boy's the result of an affair."

Her mother bowed her head, with tears running down her cheeks. "Please go, Daniela. Please, for the love of God, I cannot do this now."

Daniela's face softened, a sense of guilt permeating her. She didn't want to put pressure on her mother after what she'd been through with her father. The poor woman deserved a peaceful life, and she wasn't helping. Maybe she'd give her time to process her question and try again next time. Perhaps Rafael could use his research skills to find answers. "Okay, Mum. I'm sorry to upset you. I am leaving." She opened the door and hurried to her car, an uneasy feeling in her stomach.

Chapter 32

FLAMENCO SHOW

Rafael sat outside a bar, waiting to meet a man named Nicolas. After digging deeper, he had discovered that Abel's friend Nicolas was retired and worked as a flamenco dancer in his spare time. Surely he would know something about Abel's final months or years. Nicolas might have an idea of his state of mind at the time.

Gulping his beer, he looked around and checked his phone. The man was fifteen minutes late and Rafael had to get back to work. He wondered whether Daniela had succeeded with her mother about her father's past. There had to be someone in his life he had wronged; neither he nor Daniela had hurt anyone.

The breeze shifted, flicking hair into his eye. The weather was getting cooler as autumn approached, and he anticipated the beautiful colours of that time.

A resounding deep voice jarred him from his thoughts. "Are you Rafael?"

The man appeared to be in his sixties, with an athletic build. He nodded. "That would be me." Rafael put out his hand, noticing the droopiness of the man's green eyes, and the dark waves of his shoulder-length hair covering one of them. "Pleased to meet you, Nicolas."

Nicolas sat down and called over a waiter. "A light beer for me, please. And Rafael ..."

"I am fine. Still drinking this one." People on the street walked past them, their muffled voices drowning his thoughts. The man looked friendly enough, but would he know anything useful?

Nicolas cleared his throat and straightened. "I couldn't believe it when I'd heard that poor Abel had died. He was a good man and died too young." Rafael nodded, and the man took a breath. "What specifically would you like to know about Abel?"

"I am truly sorry for your loss, Nicolas." Rafael sighed. "I have been researching Abel's life for a series of articles I'm writing." He didn't want to lie, but he couldn't tell the man the full truth. For all he knew, he could be putting this man's life in danger. "How close were you and Abel?"

The waiter returned with his beer, and Nicolas took a large gulp. When he set it back down, he frowned. "We were close once, and he was a good man when he was sober. I pushed him to get help for his drinking, but it took him years and a lot of damage before he got to that stage. Before he realised he was hurting his family. We lost touch for many years, then he got back in contact a couple of years back. But he wasn't himself. Something had changed. He kind of seemed broken inside."

Rafael took out his notepad. "Can you be more specific?"

Nicolas took another drink. "He would come to a bar with me, and we'd be talking about sports, but often he'd be away with the fairies. Other times, he was jittery and agitated about something."

"Was he possibly worried about his embezzlement?"

Nicolas drew a hand through his unkempt hair. "No, that's where you're wrong. I do not for one second believe he would resort to embezzlement. The guy had a good heart and would never do such a thing. He was loaded, too, because of his job, so he had no need to do that."

Rafael nodded. "Sometimes people resort to such things for the adrenaline rush. The thrill of danger." Rafael wondered if Abel was innocent of the crime. Had he been set up?

"He wasn't the type to want the thrill. The man wanted peace and quiet." His eyes dampened. "I know he felt guilty for leaving his family behind. He loved his wife and daughters, but he never told me why he left. He said it had to be done, and he wasn't worthy of their love."

"Did you believe him?"

"Not for a second, but something did spook him before his death." He sipped more of his drink. "I got the sense he was in some kind of trouble, but he never opened up to me. He always said he was not worthy of anyone's love."

Rafael took a breath, knowing there was more to the story than pure self-esteem issues. Now there were more questions than answers. "Do you think Abel had any enemies?"

The man shrugged. "Jesus, I don't know. All I can tell you is that he was miserable without his family. For the life of me, I don't know why he'd leave them. It was sad to abandon them without a word, but I know he had a reason."

"Is there anything else you can tell me about his past?"

"Only that he lived alone, miserably. But if you find out anything, I'd appreciate it if you could let me know. I miss my old friend."

Rafael rose. "Of course, and thank you so much for your time, Nicolas. I'll be in touch, hopefully soon with more information."

Nicolas smiled reassuringly. "Thank you." He dug into his back pocket and pulled out two tickets. "Here are the tickets for the flamenco show, as promised. I will see you at the show next week, and hopefully you'll enjoy it."

"Of course. Thank you." He waved his hand. "I will take care of the bill." Now he had to convince Daniela to go to the flamenco show with him.

Rafael turned to Daniela after finishing their tapas and enjoying a drink from the bar. "I am sure you're going to love this, Daniela." He sat at a table beside Daniela, aware of her proximity.

"No doubt, Rafael. This was a great idea. Is Nicolas performing tonight?"

Rafael nodded. "He is, and we've got about fifteen minutes before the show, so tell me what you found out at your mum's place." He caught a whiff of her perfume but focused on their mission.

She fixed her eyes on him. "I found baby photos in my mum's garage. It was of a young boy I didn't recognise. It was an old photo, so it had to be many years old. There was no date on the photo."

"Who do you think it was?"

"My mother wouldn't tell me. She got upset and I didn't want to pressure her, so I left. I assume my father had an affair and got another woman pregnant. He must have left us for another family."

Rafael shook his head. "I doubt it. His friend, Nicolas, said he lived alone, but he didn't know why he left you and your family."

"Maybe he left his new family, too. I don't know, Rafael. Too many secrets here, and I don't know what to believe. But I know my mum's keeping a secret. I'll need you to dig further." She pulled the photos out of her bag.

Rafael stared at them. "Why does this toddler look familiar? It's as if I know this person." He stared at her as she knit her brows. "Leave it with me. I'll look into his history further."

"Tell me what you found out with Nicolas," Daniela said. Rafael took a deep breath and explained. "My poor father felt he was unworthy of us. What the hell was going on?" Her eyes widened. "What if our stalker was *his* stalker, Rafael? I always had the feeling his death was suspicious. If he was miserable without us, why did he leave us?"

"That's what we have to find out."

The lights dimmed and music blared in the background as the show was about to start. The colourful theatre backdrop was made of layers of fabric curtains. Several dancers sat on a row of chairs. A man stomped across the stage with a scowling expression, while a woman performed with flowing arm movements and the swirl of her dress to incite passion. An acoustic guitar accompanied the woman's castanets as she circled the stage with a stern expression.

Rafael watched Daniela, engrossed in the dance with her eyes lit up. He moved closer to her and stroked her hand. Their eyes locked but she didn't pull her hand away and gave him a subtle grin. His shirt felt restrictive when their arms brushed. Forcing himself to watch the show, he let go of her hand and stared straight ahead. He couldn't help having feelings he didn't want to have. Daniela's inner and outer beauty, her heart, her wit, and her strong sense of values won him over. But once they discovered the truth about her stalker, he would go back to his life and she'd go back to hers. It was how it was meant to be.

He put the photos face-down on the table, wondering whether Abel had another family he had left, too. Or had he been in trouble with someone?

He was determined to get to the truth.

Chapter 33

INTIMACY

Daniela peered out the window as Rafael drove her home from the flamenco show. She rested her head against the car seat and smiled to herself after the memorable night she had with the man beside her. The way his biceps rippled as he gripped the steering wheel, and the way one of his eyebrows rose when he was deep in thought. Even the way he brushed his tongue over his upper lip when he focused aroused her. She wanted to wrap her hands around those biceps, kiss his stubble, and do all kinds of things to his body. *No, stop it!* Their lives were in danger, and here she was having erotic thoughts about a man whom she could never have. Relationships didn't work. Men always left her sooner or later, and she didn't need more drama in her life.

Rafael touched her shoulder, breaking her away from her thoughts. She ignored the electricity shooting down her arms. "Are you all right?"

"Hmm. Thanks for the great dance show. It was out of this world, Rafael. Nicolas was great, and I wish I'd known him. He obviously separated from my dad while I was growing up." She paused in thought. "I spoke to a couple of my father's other friends, but they lost touch with him in the last six years. It was as if he alienated everyone in his life, but why?"

Rafael shrugged. "I wish I knew, but we will get to the bottom of it, Daniela." They continued in silence, and she realised that she felt safe with this man beside her. They were great as a team, and a part of her wanted to have another special night with him. As friends.

Rafael broke the silence. "Maybe we can do this again another time." Daniela's heart soared. "As friends." Daniela nodded, savouring the idea that they could at least remain friends once this was over. "I'd like that. Very much." She could have kicked herself for saying those last two words. She didn't want to give him the wrong idea.

"Great." He looked straight ahead again. "I will do some research at work tomorrow during my lunch break, and see what I can find out about your father's history. If he does have another family out there, I will find them. Don't worry."

Daniela took a breath, noticing a set of high beams behind them. She looked over her shoulder and realised the driver was tailing Rafael, inching close to his car. "That driver behind us. He's really close."

Rafael nodded. "Yeah, probably some drunk. I'll speed up and get some distance. The driver's got the damn high-beams on, too, and they're blinding me." He accelerated, but the driver behind caught up. Rafael floored the gas pedal and turned hard into a street that led towards Daniela's house. The other car followed and started flashing its high beams. "I will lose this guy, Daniela."

"What if it he's a drunk or someone who wants a thrill?"

He glanced at her briefly as his speed increased. "Do you honestly believe that?"

"What if we stop and confront him together? It's two against one. If it is the stalker, we can finally face him. If it's not, we can report the guy for reckless driving."

Rafael pursed his lips, shaking his head. "No way I am stopping. We don't know who this person is or whether he's got a weapon on him. I will lose him, don't worry." He didn't sound convincing, but Daniela went along with it.

The car behind them slowed down, then sped up. Again, it slowed, falling back before racing closer. Daniela hoped the driver wouldn't smash into them. Rafael kept his speed up, zigzagging across lanes until there were a few other cars between his and their pursuer. Then he pulled into a side street and slowed to a reasonable speed.

Looking back, Daniela didn't see the pursuing car behind her. "I think we've lost him."

Rafael stopped near a park. "Let's wait here for a few minutes. Is Blanca home tonight?" He turned off the motor but kept the radio on low.

"She is home. Why?" Daniela wondered whether the stalker knew they were investigating the truth. Were they taking risks?

Rafael clenched his hands and locked eyes with her. "I want to protect you, Daniela. Always. If something were to happen to you ..."

Daniela gasped, her heart warming as she surrendered to his touch on her jaw. Her eyes closed as his rough fingers gently stroked her cheek and the outline of her lips. It was arousing and she yearned to wrap her arms around him. The radio began to play a Spanish ballad, immersing her in the lyrics and soothing voice.

"I will keep you safe." Rafael cupped her chin and inched closer to her. He pressed his lips gently on hers. Their tongues danced in circles and their breathing grew heavier as his hands trailed the curve of her breast. Moaning, she reached out and stroked his thigh. He kissed her neck and caressed her bare leg. "Oh, Daniela. I want you so much."

Daniela brought her mouth back to his lips and kissed him deeply. She breathed heavily, tingling where his fingers brushed up and down her leg and breast.

The sound of a car whizzing by broke the momentum, and Daniela realised that this was the wrong place and the wrong time to be having sex. She hadn't had sex in a car for years and didn't want to go back to that. Her arousal had overridden her reason, but now she was rational.

She pulled away and cleared her throat. "I think we can go now." Daniela looked out the window. "The driver's gone, so we should go."

Rafael touched her arm. "Of course." He started the car and drove to her house.

Ten silent minutes later, he dropped her off at the curb. "I will be in touch, Daniela."

"Thanks again," she said. As she walked up the driveway, the sound of a speeding car behind her sent a prickle of fear down her spine. Had the pursuing driver found them? She turned to see a car, lights blinding, roar up the driveway. Daniela screamed as the car came straight towards her.

Chapter 34

POLICE REPORT

R afael's heart clenched as he threw open the door, his body quivering as he raced to Daniela. She dropped to her knees, arms over her head. The car stopped within inches of her, then suddenly reversed off the driveway and sped away.

Rafael dropped beside Daniela and wrapped his arms around her, lifting her face to his. "Dear lord, Daniela. Are you okay?" His hands traced her cheeks, the corners of her eyes, and her scalp. "Are you hurt? Talk to me."

She shook her head, her hands shaking in his hand. "I'm fine. Just scraped knees, that's all."

He helped her stand as the front door light came on and Blanca rushed out, wearing a dressing gown. "What in blazes happened? Daniela?"

Daniela rushed inside the house without answering. Blanca looked at Rafael curiously before beckoning him inside. He scanned the street but there was no sign of the car. As he walked into the kitchen, he called the police and reported the incident.

"What did you do, Rafael?" Daniela demanded when he disconnected.

He glared at her. "You could have died; don't you realise that? I don't care what that bastard said about calling the police. He is not getting away with it this time. The police are on their way."

Blanca stood cross-armed. "What's going on here? What just happened? I heard a car skidding, but I didn't see anything." Rafael explained the incident. Blanca turned to Daniela. "And why didn't you want him calling the police? Did something more happen with your stalker?"

Rafael sat across the table from Daniela. Blanca paced the floor. "The less you know, the better," Daniela answered, leaning forward. "This bastard threatened to hurt my family and friends if I went to the police, and I can't allow that."

Blanca stiffened. "I am your best friend, Dani. Please do not shut me out. I would never have shut you out when I was staying in Brazil, with everything that happened."

Rafael wished he knew the details about what had happened in Brazil, but it was none of his business. At least she was now happy with Carlos moving to join her in Madrid. "Tell her, Daniela. She lives with you and has a right to know."

Daniela's body drooped, as if in defeat. "The bastard kidnapped my sister." She explained the details.

"Dear God, Dani. Is Eva all right?"

"She is fine, now. It was only his sick game. He beat and bruised her, and he wanted to put me on edge. He threatened to kill her if I told the police, so you need to keep this to yourself." Blanca nodded. "I found out a few other things, but until we know what's going on, I don't want to risk telling you anything."

Blanca approached Daniela and hugged her tightly. "I love you, Dani and I'm here for you. Let's bring this guy down together."

Daniela shook her head, scowling. "You are not getting involved in any of this, Blanca. Please leave it alone and let us handle it. This stalker's got Rafael and me involved."

Blanca sighed. "I live with you, Dani, and we're best friends, so I *am* involved."

They argued for the next twenty minutes until the doorbell rang. Rafael opened the door to admit two police officers.

"I am Officer Gomez," said the first, a stout, middle-aged man. "And this is Officer Fuentes. You reported a car incident?" Rafael nodded as he ushered them to the kitchen and introduced them to Blanca and Daniela.

"Can you please tell us exactly what happened, and if you can describe the car in question?" Officer Fuentes asked. He was slim and appeared to be in his twenties.

Rafael gave his version of events and Fuentes jotted down notes on a pad.

"Did you see the driver?" Gomez asked.

Daniela swallowed. "The car had tinted windows, so I couldn't even tell if it was a man or woman."

Rafael wanted to reach out and hug her all night to keep her safe.

"Any known enemies?" Daniela shook her head. "Has something like this happened before? Or have you fought with anyone—an ex-boyfriend or husband, perhaps?" Gomez asked.

"No, Officer. Nothing like this has happened before, and I get along with everyone. But ..."

Rafael intervened. "Someone was following us home, but I lost him on the way." He gave them the details, then added, "We reported stalking a while back. We gave the police documents and certain text messages."

"Right. We'll look into that." Fuentes cleared his throat. "We'll check traffic cameras at the time in question for automatic plate recognition. We might be able to get the identity of the driver. But if the car's stolen, that will be a problem." He turned to Blanca. "Did you see anyone suspicious lurking around before the incident?"

"No, Officer. I was in the house when I heard the speeding car, but didn't see anything or anyone. I wish I had."

"We've contacted forensics and they'll be checking the tyre tracks and any security cameras in the area. If we find anything, we'll be in touch," Gomez said. "But in the meantime, Ms Lopez, I suggest you not go anywhere on your own and keep your boyfriend with you at all times."

Daniela cleared her throat. "He's not my boyfriend, Officer. Just a friend." Rafael felt a hammer hit his chest but brushed it off. Why did that statement hurt him when it was true? It was the way she had said it, he realized. Could she not even imagine the idea?

The officers went to the front yard to take photos. Soon, a forensics van arrived, and the crew went to work.

Rafael sighed. It would be a long night.

Chapter 35

A DISCOVERY

The newsroom was nearly empty, with several journalists chasing leads on a huge crime story. Emilio was busily talking on the phone, and the few others left were in the conference room. It was a perfect time for Rafael to research deeper into Abel Lopez. He didn't want his colleagues asking uncomfortable questions.

Rafael had searched for information when writing Abel's previous profile, but he might have missed something. Fernando, aware of the stalking situation, had approved his research on Abel. "So long as it doesn't interfere with your day-to-day duties," he had said.

Rafael thought of Daniela, and her near-miss by that crazy driver. His heart had felt like it would explode out of his chest, and he realised he couldn't imagine a life without her. He didn't want to think he might be falling in love with Daniela, but in that moment between life and death, he thought he would die of heartbreak himself. And that kiss they shared. It was magical. Like nothing he'd ever experienced before, and he wanted more. She was like a drug to him, but he didn't want to jeopardise their friendship. They were now on a mission, and had to work together.

Taking a deep breath, he began with a general web search with Abel's full name, vocation, date of birth, date of death, and any previous interpersonal conflicts. He got a number of hits, mostly information he already knew. He added further details in his search, including children and family, but again found nothing new. Social media sites only gave general information about financial awards received and his extensive qualifications.

He tried a database the newspaper used for deeper background checks, going back thirty-five years to find any other children, but there was no record of Abel Lopez having any other children nor being married to another woman. Wondering about the baby in the photo, he had an *aha* moment. What if the baby had been given up for adoption or put into foster care? That could be the only explanation.

If Daniela's parents had actually given up a child, this could be a ground-breaking article—one that could also hurt Daniela deeply.

He searched for child welfare agencies and foster care-givers, then called his friend, Leandro, a detective in the Madrid police department. He waited, tapping his fingers on his desk. "Hey, Leandro. I need a favour."

He chuckled. "Why am I not surprised? I thought I've given you enough favours to last a lifetime. What is it?"

He took a breath. "I need you to talk to a couple of residential care agencies so I can get around privacy laws. I am looking for someone who was in foster care as a child, and I am thinking he could be dangerous and after Daniela and me." He explained the series of events so far.

"Come on, man. You know there is no probable cause for us to access that information, or for those workers to disclose private details. A judge will not sign off on any warrant for this information. We could get into serious trouble here, Rafael. Breaking laws."

He had to convince his friend, knowing he could be discreet about whatever information he uncovered. "Listen, Leandro. I don't plan to publish any article with this information. We just need to know who this young kid was and if he matches Daniela's stalker, and possible killer of her father. It is about self-preservation. Her mother is tight-lipped about the past. I am sure these workers at the agencies will not say anything if we tell them it is top secret."

He sighed. "Fine, Raf. But on one condition."

"And what's that?"

"I am coming with you to make it look more official. If there is something about this kid and he is dangerous, I will need to get the detectives involved. You cannot do this on your own, bro."

"Okay, but this same guy might have been the one who kidnapped Daniela's sister, and he didn't want the police involved. We need to keep this quiet for now."

"Send me the details and I will make the appointment and explain the importance of the information."

Rafael ended the call, texted his friend the details before resting back against his chair, and pondered with his hand resting against his chin. He wondered whether her older sister knew anything, but as he could be wrong about this, he would not bother her. For all he knew, the baby might have been a boy they cared for on a temporary basis. But to have another photo of that same child as a toddler meant it was doubtful they cared for him short-term.

He needed a break so went to the staff room. He made himself a cup of coffee, and as he sipped, saw a folded note someone must have dropped on the floor. Unfolding the note, he read: *Fernando: Meet me at the hotel. Let's make a plan. It will be our secret.*

What was this?

Later that day, Daniela and Rafael went to a small building in the centre of Madrid. His friend and detective, Leandro, stood outside the residential care centre with his hands on his bulky hips. Luckily, he had worn plainclothes, wearing black jeans and a white shirt, his black crew cut enhancing his chiselled face and bright blue eyes. He approached them near Rafael's car, fixing his gaze on Daniela and nodding to Rafael. "Hello Daniela." He leaned forward and shook her hand. "I am Leandro. I gather Rafael has spoken about my work with him and the newspaper?"

She nodded. "Yes, he has. Thank you for doing this. I know it's against the rules but if we are right about this person, we can discreetly get the police involved later."

"Of course, but let me do the talking at the start." He faced Rafael. "Zip it for now."

Rafael put up a hand. "I hear you, Leandro. You can start the conversation, but I am asking questions later."

As they crossed the uneven concrete path, three young boys rushed out of the door and started kicking a ball around. A tall lady whose hair was tied up in a bun followed them. "Jose, do not push others, please. And stay in the grounds." The woman turned to Rafael and Daniela with curiosity. "You must be the detective, Leandro. I am Luciana."

He nodded then pulled out his badge. "Good to meet you, Luciana," said Leandro, and turned to his companions. "This is Daniela, who is Mr. Lopez's daughter. And Rafael, the journalist."

"A pleasure," said Daniela.

Rafael shook her firm hand. "Pleased to meet you."

Luciana's eyes flickered over to the boys, who continued to kick the ball around. A younger woman came outside and nodded to Luciana, who then led them inside the centre, to an office with bare walls, rickety-looking chairs, and a weathered desk piled high with documents. "I do not normally disclose confidential information, but you explained on the phone how you believe this child might have killed Abel Lopez, and committed other crimes?" Luciana asked.

"That's correct," said Leandro. He leaned forward in his chair. "This is a sensitive matter and a discreet investigation, which is why for the purpose of safety, we need to keep this visit quiet. It is a matter of life and death, and I promise you that this information will not impact you in any way."

Luciana's hands fidgeted and she swallowed. "I am focusing on the bigger picture here, knowing it is for the greater good, and I am hoping you will not publish any information you find here today. I understand this is purely for your ongoing investigation into Abel Lopez's past. And I wouldn't be doing this if I didn't have some concerns about a few of the residents from the past."

Leandro nodded. "I understand. We will exercise discretion. Thank you."

Rafael cleared his throat. "This child might be a murderer as well as a stalker, and we will keep this on the down-low."

"Of course, but I must warn you that back then, and even now at times, we would have worked with 'at risk' children. There was no national legal guidance, and the financial constraints made it almost impossible to give them the proper care. I worried back then about the kind of life our former residents would have without the proper guidance and safety measures in place. We had social workers and a few psychologists, but we were under-resourced and had so many children with behavioural issues. Many of them were victims of domestic violence, or had parents with mental health issues who couldn't cope with a child. Nowadays, we have moved more towards specialised care institutions. There has been progress, but it is never enough."

Daniela didn't want a history lesson. She only wanted to find her brother—if she in fact had a brother. She pulled out the photos from her bag. "Do you have any information about this toddler? We don't have a first name, but we assume he was either my brother or half-brother, the son of another mother. We don't know whether he is related to me at this stage."

Luciana nodded. "I pulled out a few of the files and found several young boys with the surname of Lopez around the same time." She hefted three thick files and flipped through them with focus. "This one is a Miguel Lopez, who was twelve when he arrived here and came from an abusive environment, parental drug and alcohol issues, and conduct disorder." She rummaged through another manila folder. "Matias Lopez was ten when he got to the centre. He had gender identity issues and neglectful parents who could not cope with his sexuality. Finally, Santiago Lopez was eight years of age when he first got here, and also had conduct disorder issues, antisocial and narcissistic traits, and came from an environment of parental alcohol abuse and mental health issues." She looked up.

Rafael turned to Daniela briefly then faced Luciana. "It could be any one of them. Can you tell us if any of them was particularly bright and could be manipulative or passive-aggressive?"

Luciana nodded. "Both Miguel and Santiago were bright and would be nice to others only when they wanted something. Both moved on to family foster care after changing their ways and behaving more according to the social norm." She picked up the phone. "I spoke to a foster carer who is willing to help out with this investigation too. Let me ring her." She made the call. "Yes, Valentina. It's Luciana here." As she turned away from them for the phone conversation, Daniela's mind reeled at how close they were to finding this young boy.

Leandro leaned forward after she ended the call. "Do you have any information about the birth parents of either boys?"

"I don't have that information at my disposal, sorry," said Luciana.

Leandro frowned and turned to Rafael, as if he started to wonder if one of those boys was her stalker. "What about propensity to violence from either Miguel or Santiago? Do you see them as hurting anyone?"

Luciana held her hands together tightly, her eyes wistful. "I started in a lower position just before these children left, and I was very concerned about Santiago's behaviour. I always worried that either Santiago or Miguel might have the tendency for violence. But without facts, I couldn't take it to a higher level. My intuition wasn't enough to speak up about it. It's possible that either one of them could be violent, I suppose."

"Can you tell us their hobbies, or what their interests were in the centre?" Rafael asked. He turned to Daniela with light in his eyes.

Luciana frowned and leafed through each folder again. "I noticed Santiago's odd behaviour over time in his last few weeks at the centre. He seemed to like control in everything he did, particularly with his interests. It was as if he had to win at all costs." She took a breath. "Miguel enjoyed sports and science and was a computer geek. Santiago liked maths and science, and was an expert with computers. But in particular, he enjoyed crossword puzzles and solving problems through cryptic clues."

Oh, Christ! Chills ran up and down her spine. It had to be Santiago.

Chapter 36

A DEATH

Daniela gazed through the car window as they drove into Centro, approximately ten minutes from the Madrid residential centre they'd just visited. Leandro left when he was called to an emergency.

She barely noticed as they passed the grand Royal Palace, the Prado Museum, the Botanical Gardens close to Retiro Park, and the Gran Via shopping strip in Centro. The walking families reminded her how her father had taken her to the Prado Museum and told her stories about the history of the artists. That was during better times.

She thought back to Luciana's comment about Santiago, and knew without a doubt that he was either her brother or half-brother. So far, she'd found no evidence of Abel having had another family. Her father hadn't left them for another woman six years earlier. But then why *had* he left? Brushing aside these thoughts, she resolved not to speculate. It was all conjecture until they gathered more information.

Rafael parked in front of a house. As they stepped out, she noted the concrete fence and steel gate, white-rendered, brick veneer with a grey roof, well-kept front garden, towering pine and oak trees, and short, green lawn. Large colonial windows gave the house a cosy feel.

The gate opened with a squeak and the concrete path was uneven. Rafael rang the doorbell. They locked eyes as they waited. He shuffled his feet and placed his hands in his pockets as if he was concerned about what more they would find.

A woman who appeared to be in her fifties opened the door. Her warm smile revealed buck teeth. "Hello. You must be Rafael and Daniela. I'm Valentina, the foster parent. Come on in."

Daniela followed Rafael down a narrow corridor, past a room where several young children and teenagers were watching a TV show. The floors were scuffed, and nails without pictures hanging from them protruded from the walls.

In the living room, Daniela took in well-matched furniture, a small flat-screen TV hanging on the wall over a scratched console unit, and two bookshelves in the corner filled with children's and young adult books. The worn and stained blue carpet was almost hard beneath her feet. The interior needed restoring.

Daniela clasped her hands as she sat on the orange, weathered couch beside Rafael while Valentina sat on an armchair. "Thank you for seeing us, Valentina."

"It is a pleasure. I don't often get to speak about Santiago Lopez, but fire away with any questions you have."

Rafael took the lead and leaned forward. "Can you give us a bit of a background about him: his age, interests, personality, and how he got along with the other children."

Valentina's eyes lit up. "I remember most of my special and bright children, and he was a hard one to forget." Her eyes peered into the distance. "Let's see now. He was highly intelligent, and the type who could solve problems among the other children. He was a mediator of sorts." She rested her hands on her lap, pondering. "He could be manipulative when he needed to get his way. I think that made him a loner. He enjoyed video games and crossword puzzles, and..." She had her eyes drawn down as if remembering. "He didn't like sports or group games, preferring to be on his own, but he behaved. When he came to the house, he was twelve and stayed until he was sixteen. After an unfortunate accident, Santiago seemed to be traumatised and said he needed to go somewhere else because of the memories. But he only stayed with the other family for two years."

Daniela's body grew cold. "What happened?"

Valentina took a breath and shook her head. "My husband, God rest his soul, died. He had a sudden heart attack in bed, which was a shock. He'd always been healthy."

The room spun around Daniela and her vision blurred. She forced her focus back to the room. Rafael reached for her hand and gave her a reassuring smile, possibly thinking the same thing. Valentina's husband had died just like her father. It could not be a coincidence.

Rafael leaned back in his seat. "Do you know where he went after he left this place?"

The lady shook her head. "No, sorry. He got a big send-off at eighteen. He said he had plans to get wealthy. I didn't doubt that. He was extremely smart and capable. But it was a shame about Luciana's brother, too."

Daniela's body jerked forward. Not another death. "What happened?"

Valentina put a hand over her mouth. "I'm sorry. I thought she would have mentioned her brother." She flailed her hand. "Oh, never mind."

Rafael intervened. "Valentina. It's important we find Santiago as he is part of an investigation. We need to know everything."

Valentina nodded. "Yes, Luciana did mention that." She frowned. "Luciana and I go way back, and I knew her brother, Samuel. He was not a very nice gentleman, and could be quite dominating with the children. He helped at the centre a few times when she needed a firm hand with the more troubled children. Santiago was one of them, and a few others too. He'd used his fists one too many times. A week before Samuel died, one of the boys hit him hard, and her brother cooled down after that. I believe he got scared to use his fists, but he still verbally abused the children. Luciana tried to get her brother to calm his anger. She even told him to stay away, but he never listened. He died in his bed of suffocation, apparently smothered by a pillow. The police investigated and questioned the children, but they never solved the case."

"The parents didn't find any fingerprints or DNA around him?" Rafael asked.

Valentina shook her head. "No, it was all clean and neat. Too neat."

Daniela wondered if it had been Santiago. "Who do you think killed him?"

Valentina clenched her hands. "I don't know. All the children hated him, so take your pick. But I often wondered if it was Santiago, as he would have had the smarts to do this and keep it clean. But I don't want to accuse him if he's innocent. Please don't assume anything without the facts."

Rafael frowned, cross-armed. "Of course." He briefly looked at Daniela whose face had turned frozen. "Do you know where he might be now?"

"I do know he was planning to move overseas to start up his own company. And he also mentioned researching Segovia as a nice place to live. But it's been about seventeen years since he left foster care, so he could be anywhere."

Daniela straightened. "Do you know anything about his family background, or why he was placed in foster care?"

Valentina shook her head. "That information has been sealed, so I don't know."

Rafael rose. "Thank you so much for your time. We appreciate it." Daniela smiled at Valentina, her legs unsteady beneath her.

"It was a pleasure, and I do hope you find him. I worry about my boys, and what has become of them."

"Of course," said Daniela. If Santiago was manipulative and passive-aggressive, it was understandable that Valentina would be concerned about them, particularly Santiago.

Chapter 37

A NIGHT AT THE BAR

Daniela rubbed her hands together as she typed out invoices for dance class the following Friday. She clicked the print button, then began stuffing the papers into envelopes she could hand to her students.

It felt good to be back in her familiar office. Most of the building was restored, and the fire inspector had given her the all-clear to return.

Rafael had invited her out for a late dinner to celebrate her return to her building. A tingle spread throughout her body as she thought about his support, and help to find Santiago. The next thing she needed to do was talk to her mother again. She had been putting it off for fear of the truth harming more than helping.

The police had contacted them about the driver who had chased them, but only to say that the car had been stolen, and there was no way to track whoever did it. They could tell her it was the same car which nearly ran her down in her driveway.

It was almost time for the next class, but Sofia hadn't arrived. Where was she? If she didn't show up soon, Daniela would need to merge two classes.

As if she'd summoned her presence, Sofia swung open the door and huffed. She put a hand to her chest and bent forward. "Sorry I am so late. Diego had a few issues to deal with at work, and seeing as my car's getting repaired, he had to drive me here." She looked back. "Oh, he's here now. He wanted to say hello." She took a breath. "I'll go stretch." She rushed off as Diego arrived at the door.

"Hello, Daniela. I wanted to say how exciting it is to come back here. You must be grateful to have your building back." His eyes glowed as if he was happier about her school than she was.

"Of course. I was struggling in the other building, but I wanted to keep the classes going. It was important for the kids to keep practising."

He nodded. "I understand, and I am going to miss seeing Sofia's friends and this amazing city. I will be going back to my home soon. I have many innovative plans in my work. A number of inspirational engineering projects which will be amazingly powerful."

Daniela didn't know anything about engineering, but his face glowed. "Sounds interesting."

He leaned forward, his musky scent prominent. "I was wondering if I'd be able to video your class for my nieces back in Barcelona? As I mentioned, they do have an interest in dance, and this will inspire them further."

Daniela knew this could be great advertising for her business. "I will need to get permission from the parents first and will let you know. Which class? Mine or Sofia's?"

He pointed to her. "How about your class?"

"I will let you know soon." She got up and straightened out her papers. "But before we go, can you help put these into envelopes? I need to hand them out to the students."

"Of course. I'd be happy to help you with those invoices."

Daniela smiled. "Thanks, Diego."

He exhaled. "It's my absolute pleasure." Then they got to work, placing the invoices inside the envelopes.

Later at the bar, Daniela rested in a padded chair, sipping on sparkling strawberry wine. Crossing her legs, she displayed a bare thigh. Her red silk dress had a split on one side, a tight waist, and a deep decolletage. It wasn't that she wanted to make an impression, but more about having fun and forgetting about her troubles.

The bar was smoky and crowded. Patrons sat at round glass tables, drinking and chatting in groups. The floor was sticky from spilled drinks. On a stage at the far end a pianist played jazz. A stocky, bearded man nearby ogled her. She turned away and faced the bartender.

She hadn't spoken to Rafael about the next step in their research, but she knew they'd speak to her family about their discoveries. They might open up to Rafael. She realised she needed to give her mother the whole truth. Then surely, she'd open up about the past.

The bearded man came up, knocking into her, but another voice interrupted him. "Excuse me, sir." Rafael pushed between the man and Daniela. Her heart skipped a beat at the way he eyed her from head to toe, as if he was drinking her in, savouring every inch of her body, his eyes stopping at the dip of her cleavage. Rafael took a breath and sat beside her while the bearded man stormed off, in search of another victim. "You look beautiful, Daniela. Mesmerising." He blushed and cleared his throat, then turned to the bartender. "A light beer, please."

"You look dashing yourself." Rafael wore a tight white cotton shirt which showed his abs, and grey pleated pants that accentuated his muscles and toned legs.

He drank his beer, then leaned close. "Tonight is about fun. No talk about Santiago or anything else. We get to have respite at this bar, and it's about us getting to know each other better." She gave him a strange look. "As friends."

Daniela nodded. "As a friend, tell me a bit more about your family. You know a lot about me, so I'd like to know about your family."

Rafael hesitated and stared into his lap. His brow rose and he rubbed his stubble with vigour. "That's fair, seeing as I know a lot about you. Where do I start?" He closed his eyes briefly and clasped his hands together as if praying. "I came from poverty and struggle, and I missed out a lot in my childhood. My father died of cancer when I was twelve, and my mother's been depressed and mostly suicidal for many years."

Daniela's heart clenched, thinking how hard it must have been to feel lonely in that way. She could relate to the loneliness from when her father abused them, and her mother withdrew in her shell, becoming depressed too. "I am so sorry, Rafael. How is your mother now?"

His eyes glistened. "She is much better, because I encouraged her to get help. But I miss my dad every day. He was one of a kind, and loved my mum and me very much."

"No siblings?"

"No, I'm an only child, and that was lonely. Growing up poor because my dad was always sick and my mum had to care for him, or work herself, meant I missed out on birthdays, get-togethers, school events, and even extended family celebrations. It was the rarest of occasions when we went to dinner out or see a movie. My friends gave up on me, and I ended up being lonely throughout high school." Before he could continue, he picked up his phone from the counter and stared at it for a minute. Something was bothering him.

"What is it?"

He looked up at her and forced a smile. "Just a work thing."

Daniela downed her drink and wondered what in heaven's name was on his phone. If only she could read his mind. Only with his intermittent stares at her leg could she guess what was on his mind, but she would not go there. Brushing aside the concern, she planned on enjoying herself tonight, and would not read more into things.

Chapter 38

TWO HEARTS

Rafael swallowed hard as he considered the text message he just received: *Stop digging or you will regret it.* He wanted to be truthful with Daniela, but he did not want to spoil this night with her. Besides, she didn't need to worry more than she already was. Especially when it was possible that her own brother was stalking them, playing a dangerous game of cat and mouse, with his cryptic clues and crossword puzzles.

He put aside those thoughts to focus on Daniela's legs, which he yearned to run his fingers over. The way the figure-hugging dress shaped her curves and dipped at the middle of her chest aroused him like he'd never been aroused. He was taken in by the way she showed her strength through challenges, and the way she enjoyed life's moments without over-thinking them. He couldn't stop thinking about her, day and night, and wanting her. It might not be the smartest thing to think about, but if his life was in danger, he might as well savour his last moments on earth with this special woman.

"Penny for your thoughts, Rafael."

Rafael gave her a reassuring smile and squared his shoulders. Her eyes seemed to brighten underneath the soft, low lighting, as if she had cat's eyes. It was mesmerising. "Let's focus on you now. Apart from running your dance school and enjoying crossword puzzles, what else do you like to do?"

Daniela smiled. "Oh, that's easy. I love yoga, going to the gym, and going to places like this where I can let loose and forget my problems."

"So you take care of your body through the gym and your mind through yoga. I can see that you work out." His eyes ran down her body again. Daniela blushed and rubbed the base of her neck. Even her throat reddened. He realised he shouldn't have said what he said, and quickly changed the subject. "I enjoy the gym too, but these days I don't get much time. When do you fit it in?"

"During the day, at least twice a week, but lately I haven't had time. And you know why. I guess dance has been my exercise lately. It keeps me sane."

Rafael licked his lips. "I loved your performance at that club. You have a lot of talent. Do you regret giving up dance?"

"Sometimes, but I get to do the occasional dance gig and that gets me by. I love teaching dance a lot more because that is steady work. Dancers don't always get to work, and I need a regular income."

"That makes sense. How about a top-up of your wine?"

"I would love that. Thanks." He signalled the bartender and ordered two more drinks, then focused on Daniela's fresh scent and light breath. If he got any closer, they'd be wrapped in each other's arms.

When an hour had passed, Rafael looked at his phone. No more messages, thank God. But he was damned if he would let this creep ruin his night. He was here to enjoy his time with Daniela, and she would be his sole focus. "It's midnight. How about a coffee at my place? I have some great music and ballads we can listen to, if you like Bruno Mars."

Daniela flinched and rubbed her arms as if she was cold. Putting on her jacket, she rose too. "I like the singer, but I don't know ... it is late."

Her eyes fixed onto his as if wanting to read his mind.

"It's just coffee, Daniela. And good music. Tonight's about fun, remember. No worries, no troubles. Just respite from all of it."

She nodded. "Right. Of course. Fun. And I enjoy music. It looks like we have the same tastes. Do you have any music by Dua Lipa or Sam Smith?"

"Of course. Let's go. You can follow me in your car."

They headed into the cool night air. Rafael gunned his engine and waited for Daniela to catch up with him. It took a half-hour to reach his home.

When he opened his door, Daniela gripped her clutch tightly. Her lip trembled, but it wasn't that cold. He prodded her towards the living room, and showed her the playlist on his iPad. Plugging the device into a sound system, he played Bruno Mars' *Leave the Door Open*. "How about a dance before coffee?" He put out his hand when Daniela nodded. She took his hand and he swayed slowly to the music while his arms wrapped around her waist. He massaged the small of her back and Daniela tightened against him, her thumbs making circles on the back of his neck. His body responded as their eyes fixated on each other. They immersed themselves in the ballad, oblivious to the outside world. He couldn't help but think he was falling deeply in love with her, but he didn't want to admit that and scare her off.

"Daniela, I ... I care about you. A lot. I want to explore whether there's something between us." She remained silent, but her eyes told him what he wanted to know. He leaned in and lifted his hand to stroke the corners of her lips, then the bottom and the top. She moaned as he trailed kisses across her neck to the base of her throat. As his mouth dipped down to her chest, she caressed the back of his head until he rose, parted his lips and dove deep into her mouth. Slowly circling his tongue, he savoured her sweet taste and scraped her lower lip between his teeth. "I want you, Daniela. So much."

Daniela dug her nails into his shoulders, gripping him tighter as his hands played with her round buttocks and pressed her harder against him. He pulled down her zipper and watched her dress slip down to the carpet. His eyes widened at the beautiful sight before him, wearing a black thong and a skimpy, strapless black bra. His mouth watered with desire. He led her to the couch and gently lay down over her. His hands outlined her breasts. He kissed her hungrily and deeply as she pulled down his zipper and stroked his penis from the top down to the tip. He was about to explode with arousal.

He pulled down his jeans and threw them to the floor. He traced her erect nipples underneath her bra, then unclasped it. He took each breast in his mouth, tantalising her with his tongue as he swirled and sucked and nipped until she made guttural sounds of pleasure. He reached for her thong, pulled it down and stared at her mound. His fingers stroked and probed her inner thighs, becoming more aroused by her wetness as she lifted her body towards him. She ran her fingers through his hair while his hands dipped deep into her mound and his tongue reached her mouth again.

He picked up his jeans and pulled out a condom from the pocket. After putting it on, he kneaded her breasts and bit her bottom lip. Knowing she was ready, he pushed two fingers inside her. He lay on top of her and guided himself inside her, moving into a rhythm as her wetness aroused him further. She arched her back, giving herself to him as he thrust gently in rhythm with her body while he continued to caress her nipples and dig into her mouth with his tongue. The thrusts deepened until spasms of desire shot through their bodies and they became one.

Chapter 39

INTENSITY

Daniela stretched out her arms in bed, slowly opening her eyes. She jerked as she remembered where she was. In Rafael's bed. With a quick yawn, she pulled the quilt higher to cover her naked body. Funny how she was self-conscious now. They had made love three times, once on the couch and twice more in bed. He was a skilful lover who knew how to make her feel loved in every way. The way he pleased her made her feel as if she was his world.

Daniela had had a few lovers and boyfriends over the years, but nothing compared to her night with Rafael. She had never experienced adrenaline and excitement coupled with safety and security. All were important in a relationship. But could she trust that he would protect her heart? Men had deceived her in the past, and her earliest fears led to all the wrong relationships. Could she take a risk with Rafael?

Gripping the sheets tightly, Daniela watched Rafael sleep peacefully, like an angel. She loved the way his mouth curled into a smile, the way his eyes looked upwards when he was in deep thought, and the way he whispered her name when they made love.

Rafael stirred and slowly opened his eyes. He shifted closer to her. Electricity sizzled in her chest at the way his eyes bored into hers with deep, ravenous hunger. She wanted to give in to that urge and let herself go completely. "Hi, gorgeous. You look even more amazing in daylight."

Daniela chuckled and threw her head back. "Thanks. So do you." She blushed. "What's with the stare?"

He pressed his lips together and stroked her cheek, his hand trailing down to her lower lip. "I want you. All of you again." Daniela swallowed, tongue-tied. She tried to rise, but Rafael pulled her back down. "You are not going anywhere."

Daniela lay back down as he propped himself on top of her. He swept his tongue into her mouth, tasting like mint. She wrapped her fingers around the fine strands of his hair. She didn't bother hiding her nakedness and arched her back as he dipped his mouth to her erect nipples and sucked and nipped. His fingers found her sweet spot, pushing and probing while he pressed his mouth into hers. She couldn't get enough of his body, pressing herself hard against his nakedness. Breaking free of her mouth, he trailed kisses down the middle of her chest then back to her breasts, savouring each kiss as if it tasted like a sweet dessert. Her breath hitched as he moved his head down to her belly button, his tongue dampening it, then trailing lower and lower until it covered her mound as his hands pressed gently against her hips. She closed her eyes, moaning with arousal as he tasted her, licking up her wetness and pushing his tongue in deep. His tongue tantalised her core and her inner thighs with precision and grace. His moans aroused her further as he prodded two fingers inside her, tasting her like she was his last meal. She had never experienced such heat and such a high. He was like a drug, and she was addicted to him.

When his hands reached for her buttocks to tighten her against him, she pushed herself into his mouth. He made love with his tongue as if he couldn't get enough of her. When he came up again to kiss her mouth, she tasted herself on his lips as he aligned himself with her body, feeling his erection. He glided across her body and devoured her lips. "You are so beautiful, Dani. I want all of you."

"I want you too," she said. "Make love to me, Rafael"

"With pleasure." He thrust into her hard and they stared into each other's eyes, sounds of yearning issuing from both their mouths. They moved in a steady rhythm until they cried out in climactic bliss.

Rafael said, "I love you, Daniela. So much."

She couldn't help but say it back. "I love you too." Nestling into the crook of his arm, she smiled to herself, and they lay in silence. She couldn't believe that she'd told him she loved him, but it felt like the most natural thing in the world.

Rafael played with her hair. "So you love me, too?"

Daniela blushed, struggling to say it a second time when she didn't know where this thing between them was going. "Yes, I do." She cleared her throat and rose. "How about breakfast?"

He lifted himself up too. "Sure, but can I have a shower first?"

"Of course. I'll keep it warm. What do you like?"

He reached for her hand and kissed it. "Scrambled eggs and coffee would be good." He headed to the bathroom. Daniela was about to go to the kitchen when a buzz reverberated. She looked for the source of the sound and saw that Rafael had not turned off his phone. She remembered the phone notification he got in the bar. She wondered what had put him in a dark mood. Should she check? Rafael would probably not appreciate her checking his phone. Then again, it was right here, and she had to know for their own safety. The water ran in the shower. Quickly, she picked it up and checked the display. It read, *I WARNED YOU!!!!*

Gasping for breath, she had to hold onto the head of the bed. An ache scraped her scalp. Leaving the phone where it was, she peered through the window, then scurried to the kitchen and looked through the other windows to see whether they were being watched. What the hell was the stalker warning Rafael about? Could he be in the house? No, crazy thoughts! This guy liked to play games and he had to be bluffing. She looked at the previous message on his phone: *Stop digging or you will regret it.* Why didn't he tell her?

Putting the thought behind her, she grabbed four eggs from the fridge and cracked them into a bowl, beating them before adding the mixture to a frying pan. She added spring onions, a pinch of cheese, and seasoning, and stirred it until it cooked. Turning on the oven, she put the pan inside and kept it on low to keep it warm. She flicked on the kettle and prepared the coffee when footsteps resounded behind her.

"That smells amazing," said Rafael.

Daniela took the eggs out of the oven and divided them on to two plates. She placed them on the table, set out sliced bread, a napkin, and placed his mug in front of him. "Enjoy." Keeping the text message to herself, Rafael devoured his eggs and took a bite of the bread.

"Tasty eggs. Thanks, Daniela." Eating in silence, Daniela barely tasted her food. She felt she needed to bring up the text message, but what would that accomplish? He probably would never trust her again. But then again, she had the right to snoop after what was happening.

He wiped his mouth with the napkin after finishing his breakfast. "So good." He frowned. "Is everything okay? Why are you quiet?"

Daniela didn't want secrets between them. "I know you might hate me for looking at your phone, but considering our current situation, I had to check it."

He pressed his lips together, knitting his brows. "What are you talking about?" She went to the bedroom and fetched his phone. When he tapped the screen, his face paled. "Oh, No!"

"Oh, yes! Why the hell didn't you tell me? I deserved to know."

He clenched his hands and looked past her as if wanting to measure his words. "You had no right to go through my phone, Daniela. No right."

She scoffed. "Are you serious right now? After what we're going through here, I thought you'd at least be upfront about this. I thought we were a team."

"And I thought I could trust you. Dammit, Daniela. This is my problem, not yours. He texted me, not you."

"You cannot do this alone anymore. It's too dangerous, and you can trust me. That's exactly why I checked your phone. It was you who didn't trust me."

He rose, squinting. "Do not make out that I'm the enemy. I didn't feel I needed to tell you because we need to find out who's doing this. I'm damned if I'll let a weak message get to me. He is not going to win this."

"So, you decided to play macho, and be the hero? You could have told me. We're working together on this. Why didn't you?"

"Like I said, it was my issue to bear and not yours. And I didn't want to ruin our night." He put his plate into the sink, then poured himself a glass of water. Moving back to his seat, he drank most of his coffee.

"You know what happened to Eva," Daniela said. "I won't put you at risk."

He shook his head, took her hand and brought it to his lips. "Listen, I am a big boy and can take care of myself. I am so sure this creep's bluffing and playing another one of his sick games. He is trying to keep us on the edge. I'll be fine, and we have to keep digging." He exhaled. "I will protect you, Daniela."

"Maybe we should go to the police. This is getting way out of hand."

Rafael shook his head. "And what will they do? Apart from a few messages, and the risk of telling them about your sister's kidnapping, we don't have any solid evidence. The police haven't given us any leads about who tried to run you over. That car was stolen."

"But they have more resources. If we tell them what we know, they might be able to do the rest. At least let them try."

"They are not going to waste their time, chasing something when there's been no incident. This guy is smart, and he's one step ahead of us. I think we need to go to your family and confront them, tell them what we know." He expelled a breath. "I know Leandro's been kept in the loop, but he can't look further into this with the rest of his team until he has a reason to."

Daniela nodded. "I hope you're right."

"With me there, hopefully your mother will be forthcoming. But let's go after lunch. This morning I wanted to check a few things on the internet about this guy."

She washed the dishes, and Rafael dried them. Then she showered and got ready to visit her mother and sister. They needed the truth.

Chapter 40

THE TRUTH

L ater, Daniela raided Rafael's fridge and found all the ingredients for gazpacho. She enjoyed making this summer soup, as it was made of raw ingredients with no cooking involved. She chopped up a tomato then added the other ingredients: cucumber, a green bell pepper, red onion, garlic, sherry vinegar, salt and pepper, and a touch of olive oil. The blender's roar shattered the quiet, and her mind drifted to the text message and what this stalker had in mind next. Her mother would have no choice but to tell her the truth once she explained what was happening to them.

Pushing down her thoughts, she turned off the blender, added bread to the mixture and let it sit for ten minutes. Then she ladled the soup into two bowls and set them on the table.

After two hours of staring at his laptop screen, Rafael rose from the couch and came to the kitchen. She sat across from him. "Did you find out anything?"

"This guy's a ghost. I can't find him anywhere on the system. It's going to be hard to find him, Daniela."

Daniela's chest squeezed tight. "I still don't like the idea of you not listening to those text messages, Rafael. If something happened to you, I ..."

Rafael reached out and caressed her hand. "I will be fine." He tasted the soup and his eyes lit up. "You are an amazing cook. I will have to get you to stay here full-time."

Daniela tilted her head, putting down her spoon. "Funny, but don't change the subject." He remained silent as he slurped his soup. "What else did you find?"

"I have found a few Santiago Lopezes, but not the one from the foster home. It's as if he doesn't exist, and I wonder if he went overseas like he planned. Either that, or he's kept a low profile. This guy might not even be our stalker."

Daniela shuddered, thinking that it might be better with the devil you know than the devil you don't. "Let's finish up here and see my family."

Rafael rose, leaned close and took Daniela's hand. "I love you, Daniela. I would like for us to try to have a relationship, but we can take it slow. I don't want to pressure you in any way. Right now, we need to focus on who's hurting us. We don't need to label this right this minute, but I don't want to let you go."

A part of Daniela wanted to label what they had, to be secure, but she understood they had other things to focus on. "I want to take it slow too, Rafael. And I would like for us to explore where this could go."

He wrapped his arms around her and kissed her hard, his hands in her hair.

Later that Sunday afternoon, Eva opened the door. Her eyes widened. "Hey, Dani. I'm glad you called ahead. Otherwise, you would have missed me. Rafael, good to see you. Come in."

"Thanks, sis." Daniela stepped in, looking around the empty living room. "Where's Mum?"

"In the shower, but she'll be finished soon." Eva ushered them to the couch. "Can I get you guys a drink?"

Rafael shook his head. "No, thanks. I'm good."

"No, thanks, Eva. Listen, we have something to ask Mum, but we wanted to ask you something first." Her sister nodded, and Daniela pulled out the two photos from the large envelope in her hand. "Do you recognise this baby?"

Eva scanned the photo closely. She shrugged. "I have no idea. Who is it?"

"That's the thing. I found these photos in the garage here. I can't be sure, but he could be related to us."

Eva's face paled. "What?" In that moment, their mother came in, staring at the pictures. She gripped the edge of the armchair and seemed to age before their eyes.

Daniela quickly got up and helped her mother to the sofa. "Mum, are you okay?"

Adriana remained silent, her body shaking.

"I'll get some water," said Rafael, and rushed to the kitchen. He returned with a glass, and Adriana drank it all down.

Daniela took the empty glass from her hands and put it on the coffee table. "Mum, take a few deep breaths. I'm sorry to upset you."

The house was silent for a few minutes before her mother managed to speak. "What were you doing in the garage?"

"I was trying to get information about Dad's past as ..." She didn't want to worry her mother, and had to break the news to her gently. "I am curious about this child. Who is he?"

Her mother pressed her lips together. "No one important. Just someone we babysat a few times for an old neighbour, that's all."

"I don't believe you, Mum. We know who this child is, but we don't know much about his background. We've searched him, but he seems to be a ghost."

Her mother stiffened. "Leave it alone, Dani. For everyone's sake."

Rafael touched Daniela on the shoulder. "Mrs Lopez. I think we need to tell you exactly what's been going on with Daniela and me, then you might shed light on the situation." He explained the stalking and their discovery in the foster care homes, and waited for her response.

Her mother looked at Eva, her eyes twitching as she shifted focus back to Daniela and Rafael. Taking Daniela's hand, she shuddered again. "I am so sorry, Daniela. I never wanted this family to be in any danger." She looked past her. "I will tell you what you need to know. Not because I want to, but because it might save this family. It's the right thing to do." She peered into her hands. "You do have a brother, and Santiago was in foster care, as you found out."

Chapter 41

FAMILY HISTORY

Eva stared into her hands, speechless. Daniela's heart constricted at those four words uttered by her mother, but she wasn't surprised. Hearing her mother say those words made it real.

"Why did you keep it a secret, Mum? How could you lie to us all these years?" Rafael reached out and held her hand. Eva covered her face with her hands, shaking her head.

Her mother swallowed, her eyes going to Eva, and then back to Daniela. "He had behavioural issues, Daniela, and we could no longer care for him. We had Santiago in our care for eight years, and had no choice but foster him out in hope he would get professional help."

Daniela frowned. "But he was getting help. The lady at the foster care centre said he was a great mediator and could solve problems. She said he was good for the other kids. Why didn't you get him back?" Her mother pressed her lips together, her eyes closing briefly as she got up from the chair and paced the carpeted flooring. Her breathing became erratic. "Please, Mum. Take a breath."

Her mother nodded. "It was the last straw when he tried to hurt Eva in her cot." Daniela froze as she waited. How could she not be surprised if her stalker was also her brother. "He ... he ..." Her mother paused as fresh tears poured down her face. She wiped them away and fought against them. "Santiago ... tried to suffocate Eva with a pillow. I walked in just in time to stop him." Her lips trembled. "I looked into his eyes, but they were dark pools of evil. He showed no remorse for what he did and kept denying his actions."

Eva looked at her mother, and her face turned white. "Are you serious, Mum? Is that really true? That young boy tried to kill me?"

Daniela's spine prickled with fear. Luciana's brother had died the same way, apparently smothered with a pillow. It could not be a coincidence, could it? Daniela knelt next to her mother and held her hand. Her mother gave her a sad smile.

Her mother moved to sit beside her older daughter and reached for her hand. "Oh, Eva. We didn't want to abandon our son, but we had to protect you. We had to think of you. You were less than two years old when he did that to you, and he was eight years old. A child, for Christ's sake, and he was so jealous of you. He hated you with a passion. Initially we thought it was normal sibling jealousy, but it was more than that. It was not natural. He was manipulative, claiming he was playing a game with you, and didn't want to hurt you, Eva. But I knew different, and so did your father. At that time, he wasn't drinking, and he was a loving and gentle father who tried his best with Santiago. Our son was a lost cause. Something evil lived inside him and nothing or no one could help him."

Daniela clasped her hands in front of her. "I am sorry you had to go through that, Mum. No doubt it was a parent's worst nightmare. Is that why dad drank and became abusive? Because of the guilt of giving him up?"

Her mother nodded. "It tore him to pieces when we gave him up. The guilt burned him and led him to the bottle. He couldn't cope with what we did, but he knew we didn't have a choice. We had to protect Eva, and we would not risk him staying with us."

Rafael intervened. "Were there other indications before that, that something wasn't right? I mean, you had him for eight years before you gave him away, so in that time, did he do anything else that bothered you?"

Her mother's body shook. "Too many to count, but I will try to remember them all." Taking slow, deep breaths, she closed her eyes briefly. "He played in a neighbour's yard when we were at our old house, and he fought with their son, Matias, who was around the same age. The neighbour knocked on my door and explained how Santiago had convinced her son to kill the cat. Santiago denied it, saying that Matias made the decision to kill the cat, but his mother didn't believe the story. Matias was a gentle soul, and he was heavily influenced by Santiago. In the end, Santiago lost a friend, but he continued to deny the effect he had on Matias." She lifted her shoulders. "Another time, we found our small dog wounded, and when we took him to the vet, the doctor said that the wounds would not heal and that the poor animal would suffer. We had to put the dog down." She held back tears. "Santiago would also turn your father against me, lying about things I never said. He would make trouble at school by pitting one of his friends against the other, and he would dare other children to do risky things. One time he convinced a young boy to stab himself with a pencil. After that incident, he was expelled from school. We tried two other schools, but he had issues there, too. The funny thing is that he wasn't violent so much as passive-aggressive and manipulative."

"Was he ever assessed by a psychiatrist, Mum?" asked Daniela.

"Yes, the psychiatrist diagnosed him with conduct disorder and narcissistic tendencies. He mentioned that as an adult, he would most likely show a mixture of antisocial and narcissistic qualities."

"Jesus," said Rafael. "That must have been tough to hear."

Her mother fixed her eyes intensely on him. "Do you think Santiago's the one hurting you and Daniela now? Is he getting his revenge?"

Rafael nodded. "It is possible, but we don't have any real evidence."

Eva spoke up. "The police. We need to get the police involved."

Daniela shook her head. "No, we do that, and he might kill you. He said that if we get the police involved, he will take drastic action. We have to fight him on our own."

Eva rubbed her hands together. "Mum, I have to tell you something." Daniela realised that they needed to explain her ordeal. "I was kidnapped, and Daniela found me." She explained the details. Her mother fainted without warning.

Daniela gasped and pushed herself up, gently rousing her mother while Rafael refilled her glass of water and returned. "Mum, please wake up. Mum."

When she came to, Daniela sighed with relief, feeling guilty for having put her through this. But they could no longer live with the lie.

Chapter 42

STRANGE MESSAGE

Daniela arrived at Kim's yoga centre the following Sunday, needing time away from her current situation, and to see her friends. Joining Blanca and the other women, she waved at Kim, who was setting up at the front. As she put down her bag and towel, a voice called her.

"Hi, Daniela," said Sofia. She smiled widely.

"Hi, Sofia. I'm glad you decided to join."

Sofia put aside her small towel then stretched her legs. "I think you're right about needing more balance in my life. It'll keep me toned for teaching, too. Isn't it great to have the school back?"

Daniela nodded. "It sure is. The students are happy to be on familiar ground, and I appreciate all your help in setting things up again."

"It's a pleasure, Daniela." Her phone rang. "Sorry, I have to take this."

In the past few months, Sofia had seemed spaced out, unlike her normal, chirpy self. It obviously had something to do with the issues over the break-up with her boyfriend.

Daniela turned to Kim, who wore sporting Lycra casual wear, her hair tied up in a high bun. She was suddenly conscious of her own casual gear compared to Sofia's designer sportswear and expensive sneakers.

Sofia put away the phone and resumed her position on the mat. "Oh, I am so unfit," she complained.

Kim put on calming music to start the session. Her eyes roved the class. "Let us begin by focusing on our breath, the in-breath and the out-breath. Now, place your hand over your abdomen and feel the movements of your breath." Kim recited a meditation trance and relaxation exercise before commencing. "Now resume the position of the tree pose ... that's right. Good."

After a gruelling pose that required her to balance on her arms, Daniela had to wipe her face with a towel. She panted through the entire session and breathed a sigh of relief when it ended. It was challenging, but her body felt relaxed and energised.

"That is it for today, ladies. I will see you all next week," Kim announced. The women clapped as she turned off the music, put away her towel, and headed into the kitchen.

Sofia turned to Daniela with a smile as she tightened her low ponytail. "How about we get a drink, guys?"

Daniela nodded. "I would love to."

Blanca gave her a thumbs up. "I'm in too, but let's wait for Kim. She shouldn't be long."

Soon, the four women were crossing the road to a tapas restaurant that had worn, green tile flooring. Square yellow stools stood along the bar, and wine glasses hung from a rack. A specials board lined a weathered brick wall, a large window on the side of the bar gave a view of the street, and passersby looked in as they went by.

They chose a square table in a corner with a tall vase of artificial flowers on it, and ordered mixed olives, fried baby squid, chorizo, meatballs, potato omelette, and assorted cheeses to share.

Daniela turned to Sofia as she popped a hot chorizo into her mouth. "How is Diego? Has he gone back home?"

Sofia nodded. "I'm sure he'll be back soon. He loves Madrid, and appreciated getting an idea of dance so our family back home can join up. Thanks for making him welcome."

"Of course. He seems like a nice guy. I assume he's not married?"

She shook her head. "No, he's divorced, but doesn't have children. It would have been that much harder to settle things with children. No doubt."

Blanca turned to Daniela. "And how are things with you, Dani?"

She feigned a cheerful response. "Great. I am glad to be back at work in our building, and Rafael's been helping out with things."

Kim's eyes lit up. "Hmm. Blanca mentioned that you two have become quite close. Have you two ..."

Daniela blushed. "We have, and it was amazing. But we are taking it slow. I don't want to rush things."

Blanca leaned forward, addressing the group. "He has it bad for you. I know because he's been very scattered at work. I think you're constantly on his mind, Dani. And I am glad you've found a nice guy. You deserve it after all you've been through."

Daniela changed the subject. "Thanks, but I can share the spotlight. What about you, Sofia? Are you feeling better after your breakup?"

Her hands fidgeted. "I'm fine. I have my daughter, and that is enough for me. My ex-husband is great, but I am better off single. If I decide to get serious about someone, they have to accept my daughter. We come as a package. She is the most important person in my life right now. Family is important." She rubbed her fingers over her nails. "But it's hard finding someone who can make you feel safe, because I don't trust many people. I keep getting hurt. I don't want my daughter to get attached to anyone unless he's the right guy." Her eyes darkened and she seemed to retreat to her own world for a moment. "For now, I am better off alone. I have more time to work on projects and hobbies, and it's best that way."

"You could at least have a bit of fun, no strings attached," Daniela said.

Sofia shook her head. "I have enough going on for now," said Sofia.

"But if someone sexy comes along, I am sure you will take on the challenge," said Blanca.

Kim sighed heavily and picked up her drink. "Oh, leave the lady alone."

Daniela stared out the window and watched passersby as the conversation changed to their favourite movies and books. Her phone vibrated in her bag. She stared at the display, frozen in shock. Her stalker was telling her something with his latest riddle: *How do you get the attention of someone you love? By screaming out, "I love you" loudly to someone else.*

Kim touched her on the shoulder. "Daniela, what is it?"

Daniela bowed her head and handed the phone to her. "He never stops. Always giving me riddles to tell me something." Blanca and Sofia got up and hovered over Kim, all staring at the display.

Sofia's face turned ashen. "I'm sorry, Daniela. What does that mean?"

Blanca looked at Daniela strangely. "Is he telling you that he is your brother, and you need to love him and not Rafael?"

Daniela nodded. "I'm not sure." An uneasy sensation shivered down her spine. "Let me ring Rafael." The phone went straight to voicemail. She tried again, with no response. "I'm sure he's probably busy with Fernando or doing research. I'll ring him tomorrow."

Sofia stood. "Oh, no. I just remembered, the babysitter's got to leave early tonight. So sorry, but I have to rush. And about the text.

I'm sure it's nothing for you to worry about. I'll see you at work, Daniela. Bye, guys."

Kim and Blanca waved goodbye, but Daniela sensed that Sofia was lying. *Why?* A few minutes later, her phone rang. It was Rafael, telling her he'd been in the shower.

Daniela breathed a sigh of relief. Rafael was fine.

Chapter 43

MISSING RAFAEL

The next morning, on Monday, Daniela came to the kitchen, where Blanca was pouring a cup of coffee.

"Would you like some?"

"Sure. Thanks."

Blanca placed a second mug on the table and sat beside her roommate. "Are you okay after that text last night? I know you're worried about your mother after finding out about your brother."

Daniela shrugged. "I don't know, but didn't you think Sofia was acting strangely?"

Blanca shook her head. "I think she is just shocked by your texts, and trying hard to juggle both work and her daughter."

"I don't know. I feel like she's hiding something. And even when she reassured me about that text message, she seemed more worried about it than I was. And why did she leave all of a sudden?"

Blanca tilted her head. "I hear you, but these are questions you need to ask Sofia. Consider talking to the police about this latest text message. They've already got you on record, and they have a lot more resources than you and Rafael."

Daniela sipped her coffee. Watching the steam rise, she wondered how else to proceed. If she contacted the police, would she be putting her family at risk? Or was the stalker bluffing? She couldn't take that risk. It was better to keep things between themselves.

Her phone buzzed on the coffee table. She went to the living room and read, *Sorry. Can't make it to work tonight. Family emergency. Sofia.*

Blanca rushed to her side. "Is that the stalker again?"

"No, it's just Sofia. She's not coming in to work tonight. That is a bit of a coincidence after acting strangely last night. She hardly ever takes time off. I wonder what's going on with her."

"She might be having issues with her daughter or her ex-boyfriend. It could be any number of reasons, Dani. Don't read too much into it. People do have problems."

She nodded. "I guess you're right, Blanca. But still ..." She opened her contact lists and called another dance teacher to fill in for Sophia. Then, turning back to Blanca, she said, "I've got someone else covering her classes tonight."

"What can I do to help, Dani? You shouldn't be alone in this."

Daniela held Blanca's hands. "Listen. I will be fine, but for now, please go to work. I've got this, girl." Blanca shook her head and walked away in a huff, and Daniela's chest tightened.

She returned to the kitchen, washed the dishes, and then showered. When she finished, Blanca leaned into the bathroom. "I am off, Dani. I'll see you tonight. And please ring if you need anything. Anything at all."

"I will. Have a good day." Daniela brushed out her tangles, then tied her hair up in a low ponytail. In the mirror, she saw a thinner face than normal, with dark circles under her eyes. She hadn't had much of an appetite lately, and it showed. Once this was over, she would make sure she took better care of herself.

She booted up her laptop to check her dance schedule for tonight. She had a few jazz and ballet classes to teach, but she'd be finished by nine o'clock.

She called Rafael to wish him luck for the day, but it went straight to voicemail. As she put her phone down, it buzzed again. She froze when she saw the text. *Follow the hidden clues on page eleven of crossword from "Eva's Challenge" to save your beloved.*

Daniela's vision blurred. She crossed her arms against a sudden chill. *No, no, no. Rafael is fine. He's in the shower, or still in bed.*

She called him again, but he didn't answer. She tried three more times, leaving messages to call her back. She found the books of crossword puzzles the stalker had sent, turned to page eleven and filled in the words as fast as she could. He had hidden a clue inside the puzzle, so she had to stay sharp and alert.

Number one across: Etch. She thought of synonyms. Design. No, too short. Draw. Also too short. Sketch. No. Scratch. Yes, possibly. Then she looked at the other clues: Number ten across: An admired person. That had to be idol. *Yes, it fits.* Another clue: To fall asleep: *Nod off. That fits, too.*

With the help of the internet, she completed the crossword within thirty minutes. Staring at the puzzle, she looked for the main hidden clue inside. It had to be in there, but she did not see it.

Her breathing accelerated and her legs shook. No, she could do this. She needed a break to rest her eyes. But the clue was in there. It had to be. She called Rafael again, only to hear his voicemail again. *Damn!*

What if this was a trick and Rafael was home? Should she take the risk and check on him? But if he had been kidnapped, that would waste precious time. Steeling herself, she took a calming breath, and scanned the clues again. She tried reading the words going down from right to left then left to right. Was it possible, the clue was Local Cross Catholic? Cross had to do with a Catholic church, right? And local meant it was in her local area.

Daniela dashed to her car and headed straight to the first church of several, at least twenty minutes from her house. But Madrid had many churches.

Daniela dashed to her car and floored away to another church, of several, at least twenty minutes back to her house. But Max and her worried thoughts.

Chapter 44

CLOSE TO DEATH

D aniela visited at least five churches, but found no sign of Rafael. The sixth stood tall and majestic with its large dome, balustrades in front, and sculptures on both sides. She ran, breathless, then across the grounds, scanning for any sign of Rafael.

Nothing. Only a few people were praying in each of its several chapels. Was one of them her stalker or her brother? She had no way of knowing.

The priest went out through a side door. Should she question these few people about whether they might have seen something? Or would that put Rafael in more danger? For all she knew, the creep might be holding him in yet another church. But what choice did she have? She had no other clues.

She scurried outside again. All was quiet until a lady's scream reverberated from the parking lot. Daniela rushed to the car park behind the church and spotted a young woman bent down at an awkward angle. She couldn't see anything beyond, but as she approached, her heart almost stopped. *Rafael! Oh, my God!* He had been dumped on the ground like a bag of rubbish.

The young woman stood in shock. "Is he dead?"

Rafael was lying with his right leg bent underneath the left one, his face bloodied and bruised, his hair matted with dried blood, shirtless chest crossed with superficial cuts. His ripped pants showed more bruising around his legs.

Dear god! He's been beaten to a pulp. He was breathing and his pulse was rapid. Daniela didn't want to move him in case he had a fracture she didn't see. She looked up at the woman. "Call an ambulance and the police."

The woman nodded, retrieved her phone from her handbag, and placed the call. A few passersby stopped, watching.

Daniela sat on the ground beside Rafael, scanning the church grounds. As she had checked this area when she had arrived, she surmised he'd been dumped here when she was inside the church.

She hovered over Rafael and stroked his hand. "You'll be okay. You'll be okay, Raf. Hang in there. The ambulance will be here soon."

"They're on their way," said the young woman. "Can I help?"

Daniela nodded. "Yes. The police will want to talk to you and me." The woman gave her a reassuring smile, and stood awkwardly as she watched Rafael while others looked on, whispering to their companions. "Did you see anyone around Rafael earlier?"

"No, it was quiet when I found him here," the woman replied.

A gust blew her hair into her face as she watched Rafael's shallow breathing. Her throat was dry and her body cold, despite the warmth in the air. She knew who had done this, and she would make sure that he paid. More than ever, Daniela was determined to find the psychopath, and make sure he was punished to the full extent of the law.

Picking up her mobile phone from her bag, she focused on the display and checked the time. Eleven o'clock! Where was that ambulance? What if Rafael took a turn for the worse, and he didn't make it? His breathing was so shallow. "You will be fine, Raf. Don't you dare give up. I'm here for you."

The woman neared her and touched her gently on the shoulder. She had bright blue eyes and wore a tight bun. "He'll be all right. It's only been about fifteen minutes. The ambulance will be here soon."

Daniela smiled, her breath erratic. "I know. Thanks."

As if commanded by a higher power, the ambulance turned into the parking lot. Daniela stood and waved them over. Two paramedics rushed to Rafael's side. "What happened?"

Daniela shrugged. "This lady found him like this here. He was just dumped here in this state. Help him, please."

The woman beside her trembled. "I don't know what happened to him."

"What's his name?" The male paramedic had bright blue eyes and a strong gaze. He knelt down, checked his pulse and breathing, then placed an oxygen mask over his face. "It looks like he's been badly beaten and cut, with multiple contusions. We'll need to get him quickly to the hospital to check for internal bleeding." The second paramedic, a woman with a high ponytail, raced over with a stretcher. The two gently put Rafael on it. "The police were not far behind us. They should be here any minute now," said the first paramedic as he dressed Rafael's wounds and bandaged his arms. "We'll take him to La Paz Hospital if you want to see him there later."

"Okay. I'll be there. Thank you," said Daniela.

The female paramedic said, "Here are the police officers now. They'll want to check this area for any evidence, and get both of your statements."

She waited for the police officers to reach them, watching as the ambulance left. They later told the police that they had just found Rafael lying on the ground, hoping he would recover quickly.

That evening, Daniela sat on the edge of the hospital bed, holding Rafael's hand as he slept. He had woken when the paramedics brought him to the hospital, and now they awaited the results of tests.

His facial bruises and the wounds across his body made her flinch as he awoke. Turning his head towards her, he half-smiled in pain. "Daniela ..."

She put her fingers to his lips. "Sssh. Don't say anything. I can see how much pain you're in." She read something in his eyes. Shame, sadness, disappointment. Did he feel guilty for getting beaten? "The doctor should be here shortly, but I found you near the church. You'd been beaten, Raf. Badly, so now you need to let the wounds heal. But I am with you all the way."

He nodded and slowly rose to a sitting position, grimacing in pain. "Sorry, Daniela." She waited for more. "I don't remember much. Still hazy."

She wanted to get this bastard, and kill him herself after what he'd done to Eva and Rafael. It had to be the same person, but why? What possible reason could he have to hurt Rafael? If it was her brother, then he might have been jealous of Rafael. He must have felt abandoned with evil intent, given he'd been diagnosed with narcissistic tendencies and antisocial traits. She had to find out who was doing this.

Chapter 45

AN ARREST

T he day after Rafael arrived in the hospital, Daniela was still by his side, her hand warm and tingly in his own. He had failed her when he had the chance to bring this guy down. The image of his face was unclear but familiar, and he knew he'd remember in time.

A doctor entered the ward, tall and chubby with stubble around his chin and droopy eyes. Rafael turned to see him, causing pain that made him wince.

The doctor carried a manila folder and opened it up. "Good morning. I am Doctor Morales. I have the results of your CT scan and it's all clear. No internal bleeding, no swelling of the brain. The mild concussion you experienced might give you headaches for a while. Do you have a headache now?"

Rafael shook his head. "Very mild."

"Great to hear." Dr Morales turned to Daniela. "He is lucky to have your support, Ms Lopez, but please make sure he does take it easy when he gets home."

She nodded. "How long before he can leave?"

The doctor cleared his throat. "Let's review in a couple of days. Those cuts on your chest are superficial, but I would still like them dressed here in the hospital before sending you home. The bruising on your legs and face will heal in time. The nurse will come by later to give you your next dose of painkillers. Any other questions?"

Daniela leaned forward. "Will he get more of his memory back, Dr Morales?"

The doctor cleared his throat again. "I believe so, but it might take a few days, at least until the pain settles a bit. Sometimes, the pain distracts the mind and can block memory, too. But rest assured, you will make a full recovery."

Rafael shifted to relieve his aching joints. "Thank you, doctor."

Dr Morales stood to leave, then turned back. "Did the police come and see you last night, Mr Martin?"

"They did. Thank you."

After the doctor left, Daniela turned to him with a questioning look. "Do you remember anything more about the attack?"

He knit his brows. "It was a man who looked familiar, but I can't place him yet." He frowned. "I will remember. I told the police what happened, and they'll look into it. Supposedly." He fixed his eyes on her. "How did you even find me?"

Her body shook. "His usual cryptic clues in his made-up crossword. I figured it out."

Blanca, Carlos, Kim, and Fernando entered the ward, greeting Rafael one at a time, their voices spiking his headache.

Kim smiled and touched her throat. Her demeanour was gentle and relaxed. "I am sorry about what happened to you, Rafael. How are you feeling?"

He managed a fleeting smile. "I am healing slowly, thanks Kim." She gave him an awkward smile and moved closer to the window.

Fernando touched him gently on the shoulder. "How are you really feeling, bro?"

"Much better, Nando. I am made of steel." His friend chuckled slightly.

Carlos rested on the other side of the bed and leaned in. "You do not look good, man. Is there anything we can do?"

"No, I'm good. Getting all the help I need, and once I get home, I'll be fine."

Blanca looked at Daniela briefly before turning to Rafael. "Do you know who did this to you, Rafael? Do you remember anything?"

He shrugged. "Nothing distinctive, but the doctor said I should remember more in a few days. I'll make a full recovery."

Fernando scoffed. "As soon as the police find this creep, I'll be writing a huge scoop about it and give you justice. He'll be finished and will be punished to the full extent of the law." He took a breath. "It has to be that stalker, right?"

"I believe so," said Rafael. "I think he's also the source I had for Abel's story, and no doubt it has to do with Daniela's father." He didn't mention anything about it possibly being Daniela's brother, as Fernando had a problem keeping secrets.

Blanca sighed. "Don't worry about any of that for now. Focus on getting better and back to bothering me at work."

Daniela chuckled. "I'm sure you're working peacefully without him, girl. You don't need this guy."

Rafael loved the banter, realising he was in more love with Daniela with each passing day. "You are so funny, aren't you, Dani?" He wanted to wrap his arms around her and make love to her.

Her eyes locked with his and lit up, oblivious to everyone in the room for the moment. "Very."

Fernando chuckled. "Get a room, guys. We are still around, you know."

Blanca threw her head back in laughter. "I can feel the heat between you both. And it is burning a fire in this room right now."

Kim touched Blanca on the arm. "You are right. It is sweet and tender."

The banter stopped as soon as two tall policemen entered, approaching Fernando. One of them had short, glossy brown hair and scars on his face. They identified themselves. "Are you Fernando Abanto?"

He knit his brows. "Yes, Officer. What is this about?"

"You are under arrest for the assault on Rafael Martin. Now you can come with us quietly or we can cuff you. Your choice."

Rafael flinched, his body turning numb. Then he remembered Fernando's heated confrontation on the phone and the note mentioning a secret. Had he been communicating with the stalker? Rafael had chosen not to confront him about the note.

"I am sorry, but you have the wrong guy," he said. "Fernando didn't attack me." Rafael didn't sound convincing, and others looked on in shock.

Fernando's eyes darkened. "I will come with you quietly." Turning to Rafael, he said, "Raf. I didn't do this. Please believe that, man."

The taller policeman with blonde hair said, "We have a credible source, Mr Martin." The group could only watch the cops pull Fernando out of the ward.

The room became tense and empty for Rafael without his friend. He could not have done this, could he?

Chapter 46

THE DREAM

Daniela and Blanca entered their home in shock, their hearts heavy. Blanca wrapped her arms around Daniela in the foyer, both of them trembling. They had just found out that Fernando was suspected of assaulting Rafael. How could that be? Fernando was his boss and friend, so what would possess him to hurt his own friend? It had to be a mistake.

Daniela sat on the couch, setting her mobile phone on the coffee table. She turned on the TV, flicking through the channels until she found a telenovela she could escape with. Blanca went to the kitchen to make tea. When she brought two cups to the living room, Daniela's phone buzzed. Her finger hovered over the screen.

Blanca sat by her side and lingered over her phone. "What's the message?"

"I don't know. I'm afraid to click on it."

Her friend took the phone and tapped the screen. "Oh Christ! What does this even mean? It can't be ..."

"What is it?" Daniela looked at her phone and froze at the GIF of a pillow with the phrase, *A parent and fragile boy.* "Oh, no! This must be Santiago. I have to tell the police about this, Blanca. It is getting way too dangerous. He's going to hurt my mum, but she's with her sister. No one's at home, but he doesn't know that, does he?"

"Let's go to the police. He might have threatened you against going to the police, but you need to protect your family. Besides, the police are already involved, and he seems to have escalated already."

Daniela nodded. "You're right. I have to tell them everything I know and hopefully they can find this creep. Fernando's in custody so he couldn't be doing this. He's been set up."

"I think you're right. Let's go."

Later that night, Daniela lay in bed, thinking about their visit to the police. They had taken her information about Santiago seriously, and explained how they would investigate her claims. She didn't know whether they would let Fernando go, but without hard evidence, they most likely couldn't hold him. At least her mother had answered, telling her that she and Eva were safe at her sister's house.

Daniela fell into sleep, but tossed and turned throughout the night, flinging the covers over her. She dreamt she was seven years old, hiding behind the couch in her parents' living room as she played hide and seek with her father. It was a good day as he hadn't been drinking. Then the phone in the kitchen rang and her father answered it. She stood up and watched him as he shook his head. When he hung up and clenched his hands, she ran towards him and pulled on his sweater. "Who was it, Daddy?"

Her father glared. "Go to your room. Hide and seek is over." He went to his bedroom. Daniela saw through the gap in the door that her mother was making the bed. Her father went in and closed the door. Daniela pressed her ear against it. Their voices were low, but she could hear a few things.

"He wants to see us," her father said.

"But why after all this time?" her mother replied.

"He said something about wanting to visit the countryside in the Basque Country. He wants us to take him there. It's where he'd like to live someday."

"But he's only sixteen, and he's already thinking about the future?"

"He's a sick, but smart, son of a bitch. We need to see him and make sure he understands that this is it. No more threats and no more visits."

"I hope we can get through to him."

When they stopped talking, Daniela rushed to her room and jumped into her bed. She wondered about the phone call and who her parents had to visit.

Later that day, her parents explained how they had to visit her father's client. They said nothing more until they left the house later that day.

Daniela woke up gasping, her heart racing and the back of her neck covered in sweat. What was that memory even about? Could her parents have been talking about Santiago? Speaking to her mother would shed light on the memory.

She rubbed her eyes and rose from bed, wrapping the dressing gown over her shivering body. Stretching out her arms, she headed to the kitchen and prepared breakfast before heading to the dance school for a Saturday morning ballet class. While driving, she called her mother at her aunt's house but got no answer on the landline, nor Eva's mobile phone. She tried again without a response, so she left messages. Then she called Rafael at the hospital to tell him about her dream.

Chapter 47

SOFIA'S SURPRISE

"**O**kay, girls. Let's do that routine again, and remember posture and legs straight. You need to breathe, too."

Daniela watched as her young ballet students twirled and glided across the room. Two knocked into each other and fell to the ground. "Luna and Ava. Please get up and stop laughing. This is a serious routine, and you need to focus on your timing. We cannot have that again." Both girls nodded and rose.

She walked around the class and decided to check on Sofia, who was teaching in the next studio. They hadn't had time to talk about the other night as she had been away from work for a few days, which she found strange when she hardly took time off. Even today, she appeared distracted, as if something was on her mind. Did something happen? And why wouldn't she tell her anything? *I'll talk to her later.* "Now, one last time before we finish." Her eyes swept the room as the girls danced perfectly. She knew that some of her students needed strong discipline and structure, but her older students needed a bit more flexibility within the dance.

Daniela continued to watch until the end of the dance. Clapping her hands, she said, "Bravo, girls. That was much better, but you still need to work on your posture in the middle of the routine. I will see you next week. Have a good weekend." The girls scurried out to their waiting parents in the foyer.

Classes were over for the day, but Daniela took a minute to get her bearings before confronting Sofia. She went to the staff room, where Sofia fidgeted while checking her phone. She looked at Daniela with darkness in her eyes. What was she worried about?

"I am glad you're still here. We need to talk," Daniela said. She brought a chair close to Sofia's desk and spoke directly. "Is everything okay with you?"

Sofia averted her eyes. "Of course."

"Are you sure? The other night you rushed out of the tapas bar, then you became anxious over that text. And you've taken time off, which you never do. Are you worried about something?"

Sofia crossed her arms, rose from the chair and shook her head. Her mind seemed to be miles away. "I am all good. It's still this issue with my ex-boyfriend. I'm still hurting, I guess. And I worry about my daughter. That's it. Usual stuff." She placed a hand on her chest as if struggling to breathe. She turned to Daniela. "I should be asking you the same thing. How are you doing with ... everything?"

"I found out something from my mother recently." She explained about Santiago. "He was fostered out because he had behavioural issues. My parents couldn't cope with his behaviour, especially when...."

Sofia angled her head. "When what?"

"My brother tried to smother Eva with a pillow in her cot when she was a child, and after that, my parents put him into foster care. They tried to get him help, but they couldn't cope, and didn't want to risk Eva's life by having him stay with them."

Sofia's eyes dilated. "Dear God! I am so sorry. How old was he at the time?"

"He was only eight years old."

Sofia's face paled. "Jesus! Your brother tried to kill Eva at that age? No wonder your parents gave him up. I would have done the same thing if my other child tried to hurt my daughter. I would do anything, absolutely anything to protect my child and my family."

Daniela angled her head. "Are you sure you're okay? It looks like you're struggling to breathe. Please tell me what's going on, Sofia." Daniela clasped her hands together, thinking how worried Sofia looked. Her eyes told her she was hiding something. "You know you can tell me anything, Sofia. We're friends."

Sofia's eyes darkened, and she stared at Daniela for a minute in silence. Scanning her phone again, she looked up at her strangely. "I think I'll get going."

Daniela's chest tightened. Her eyes scanned the room as Sofia slowly walked over to her bag and rummaged inside. What was she looking for?

Daniela felt uneasy. Why did she suddenly fear for her life? And what was behind Sofia's strange behaviour? She thought back to the moment it had begun; it was when she had first mentioned the stalker. Sophia had overreacted to the text message and flown out of the bar. She had distanced herself ever since Daniela had been stalked, and had most likely lied about needing to take time off because of her daughter. Over the last few months, she had become distant, if she had truly thought about her behaviour. She must have had a reason for these lies.

Sofia couldn't be involved in this, could she? They had been friends, and she'd been loyal over the years. But how well did she truly know her? Picking up a pen from her desk, she stood and waited for Sofia to leave. If Sofia was up to something, she would jab the pen into her eye. "I will see you tomorrow, Sofia."

Sofia sighed and pulled a knife out of her bag, the shiny glint of metal almost blinding. Sofia walked slowly towards Daniela with a blank expression on her face.

Chapter 48

HOSPITAL DISCHARGE

R afael was still reeling over his friend's arrest. He knew that
Fernando was innocent, and he would prove it. Fernando had
been acting suspiciously lately, but that didn't mean he would assault
his friend.

He pulled his laptop from the foot of the bed onto his lap and
opened a search. Daniela had called him with a revelation from her
dream, saying that Santiago liked the countryside of the Basque
Country, in the north of Spain. Rafael started searching for places her
brother might be hiding. For all he knew, Santiago could have more
bodies stashed away in a basement in the north of Spain.

Making a search for the Basque Country, he narrowed in on Bilbao
in the province of Biscay, and on Vitoria-Gasteiz in the province of
Araba and Alava. But how could he narrow it down? He was in no
state to drive for four hours, but for love he could try.

He rang his friend, Leandro, who had started working with the
detectives assigned to this investigation, knowing he'd have more
resources, or would know of anyone fitting Santiago's description,
particularly after Fernando's arrest. "Hey, Leandro. I need your help."

"Shoot," said his friend.

"I need you to make a search of regions in the Basque Country,
namely Bilbao and Vitoria-Gasteiz. Santiago Lopez might have a

house in the countryside."

"Sure, but it hardly narrows it down. But then again, if I look over the notes we got from your friend, Daniela, we might be able to narrow the search. We can follow the money trail. But aren't you still in hospital?"

He drew back. "Daniela came to you?"

"Yes. She told us about her brother possibly stalking her, but we can't let go of Fernando just yet, at least not until we've dug deeper into this. How are you feeling, brother?"

"I need to get out of here. Can you please get back to me?"

"Sure, but leave it to us. You're in no state to go travelling for several hours."

"No worries. Thanks, man."

He ended the call, then rang Daniela. It went to voicemail. He waited five minutes, then called again, but still only got voicemail. He tried twice more at five-minute intervals, but still nothing.

Rafael lay back in his hospital bed and closed his eyes with the laptop on his lap. Putting it aside, he cast his mind back to the crossword puzzles Daniela had spoken about, searching for a clue. It might have been something that Daniela missed while she was searching for Eva and himself. There was no way he'd get to the location lying here in the hospital.

He called Blanca. "Hey, it's me."

"Hi Raf. How are you feeling?"

"Much better. Listen, are you home right now? I can't reach Daniela."

"No, I'm not, and Daniela would be at work, teaching a dance class. She should be back home soon. Why?"

"Are you close to home?"

"Sorry, Raf. I am at Carlos's friend's place, having a late lunch. What is it?"

"Nothing. I just wanted a copy of that crossword puzzle to check out something, but don't worry, I've got my detective friend on it."

"If you can wait a few hours, I should be home then. Besides, you should be resting, and not worrying about any of this."

"No, it's fine, and I am resting. Thanks, and have a good time." He ended the call with a heavy heart. He had to get to that puzzle. He didn't have a key to Daniela's house, but he had learned how to pick a lock in his younger days.

Wincing in pain, he dressed. As he picked up his laptop, a stocky, elderly nurse entered the ward. "I'm here to check your temperature." She frowned. "What are you doing? You should be in bed. You are in no state to go gallivanting around, Mr Martin. Now, lie down." She pushed him back to bed, but Rafael shook his head.

"No, I have to go. Duty calls."

She scoffed. "If you are discharging yourself, we are not responsible for your wounds any longer, Mr Martin."

"Don't worry. I take responsibility for my own health, so let me out of here."

Rafael took a taxi to his house and jumped into his car. He sped to Daniela's dance school, hoping she would still be at work. Quickly exiting his car, he rang the bell on the door but got no response. The place didn't look open, so she must have been on her way home.

Getting back in his car, he drove fast to Daniela's place. He rang the doorbell but got no response, so he pulled out a safety pin from his jeans pocket and jimmied the lock until he heard a click. He pushed the door open and called out. "Daniela, are you here?" He searched all the rooms and the backyard, his heart beating a mile a minute, but she wasn't around. The back of his neck sweated, and his stomach somersaulted. If that loser had her, he had to save her. She would be okay.

He retrieved his phone from his pocket and called Daniela a few more times, but it only went to voicemail again. *Stay focused*. He began searching for the crossword puzzle and looked in the living room, the kitchen, scoured through cupboards, and finally in her bedroom. It was nowhere to be found. He looked in the laundry, then outside in the garden. Where could it be? The study. It had to be in that final room he didn't check.

There, he reached up into a high cupboard, but he only found books, manila folders, and envelopes. He searched several in-trays on the desk, underneath bills and receipts but nothing. Then he noticed a partially open side drawer. Opening it, he found it.

Quickly, he flipped through the pages in search of a clue hidden in the puzzles that Daniela had finished. He couldn't see anything, but he did sense a pattern. She had partially completed two puzzles, and the second had the title, "Final Challenge." *What!* Now he had to solve this puzzle.

He didn't have time to wait for Leandro, as it could mean the difference between life and death. He opened his phone to do web searches, and started working on the next puzzle, hoping for clues to a hidden code that would give him the exact address where the stalker held the woman he loved. This guy liked to play games, and no doubt, he would leave a clue for his next step.

Chapter 49

CAPTURED

Rafael held a pencil in his hand, studying a crossword puzzle with three clues remaining after Daniela had worked on most of it. The first clue was, "a law that hasn't yet passed." That was easy: a bill. The second clue was "A man's desire when stressed." He scrunched up his face, closing his eyes. It started with a "B." Was it breakfast? Bonus? What did he like to destress? Of course, a bar. Those two words didn't mention a location, but then he came to the final clue. This had to be it. 'The home of the Guggenheim'. He thought about that, realising it had to be the Guggenheim Museum in Bilbao. The first two clues were a smokescreen, probably meant to waste precious time. If only he'd looked at that final clue first. But Bilbao had to be where that creep was.

He tried to ring Daniela again, but she still didn't pick up. His calls went directly to her voicemail without even ringing. Strange! Her battery must have died. But he didn't have time to do anything about that—he had to get to Bilbao in the Basque Country.

He pushed the gas pedal down as he raced towards his destination, four hours away, but he didn't exactly know where he was going. It was two o'clock, so he should get there by six. He called Leandro. "Leandro, it's me. I have a place where Santiago might be."

"How did you get it so fast?"

"Never mind. I thought I'd give you a heads-up as I don't know what the bastard's planning. I need an address. Have you guys found him?"

"Aren't you still in the hospital, recovering?"

"I'm still here. Don't worry," he lied. A car behind him honked its horn.

"What the hell was that? A horn. Rafael, I hope you're not driving. You're meant to be in the hospital, man. Turn back now. We will take care of this. Stay put."

"I can't. Daniela's not picking up and I'm worried he's taken her. There is no time to wait for you guys. I need an address. Please. I will get there faster than you guys. I am already on the way. I'll hopefully be able to stall things until you get there."

"We followed the money trail that led us to this address, but it appears the guy bought it under a different name. The money Abel embezzled led us here, and we're thinking that Santiago used that money to put down a deposit to buy this place in Bilbao."

"The address, Leandro. I am closer than you guys."

"Fine." He recited the address. "But we are leaving soon; once we get the go-ahead from the sergeant, which we are doing as we speak. Hang tight and wait for us to get there. Do not confront him."

"Too late, Leandro. I have to stop this guy."

"Rafael. You are out of line here. You're a civilian and you—" Rafael ended the call and raced on. He would get there before dark, and hopefully he'd make it in time.

He had his card ready when he reached tolls so he could get back on the road quickly. After he rushed through the wine region of La Rioja, the landscape changed from semi-arid plateau to the mountains. He had to stop for more tolls, but at least the roads were mostly clear.

He passed through Navarre and headed into Alava, and then finally reached the Basque Country. In normal circumstances, the breathtaking beaches and the amazing vistas on the way into San Sebastian would have awed him, but his fatigue and the pain from his injuries made his eyelids heavy. His mouth was dry and the back of his neck sweaty. He had been sitting for almost three hours. Clenching his shoulders, he shook it all off. He would worry about his aches and pains later.

An hour later, he reached Bilbao in the middle of the mountains. He had been to this part of Spain before, with its rugged coastlines, soaring cliffs, beaches, and quaint villages, but it had been several years ago. One day, he hoped to bring Daniela here. They could have an amazing road trip, if he lived to tell the tale of his current trip over here. No, he had to believe that Santiago would be caught by surprise. He was one step ahead of the stalker this time.

His heart skipped a beat when he pulled up in front of a stone house, surrounded by billowing oak, beech, and fir trees. He would have appreciated the sloping green hills behind the houses, which would have formed a picturesque backdrop if they hadn't been behind a murderer's home.

He made certain to park his car in a hidden spot among the trees so he wouldn't be seen. He approached the white stone house on foot. It had several broad windows, and a brown roof with a chimney. A black sedan was parked in front.

He saw a smaller stone house thirty metres away and crept towards it. The door was locked, so he took the pin from his pocket to open it as he had at Daniela's home.

Looking behind and around him, he listened carefully. All quiet. He assumed Daniela was inside, and he had to get her outside the house before taking care of Santiago. He didn't have a weapon, but he had his wits about him. He could stick the pin in Santiago's eye—that could do some damage.

As he started picking the lock, a voice behind him made him shudder. "Well, well, well. If it isn't Rafael coming to save the day."

Rafael slowly turned around and came face to face with his enemy. "Diego."

His body went cold as he realised that Diego was in fact Santiago. No wonder he was like a ghost.

Chapter 50

FRIEND OR FOE

Daniela stared at Sofia gripping the knife, her eyes darting behind her employee, and then back at her. If only she could reach for her phone in her bag.

Sofia continued to approach Daniela slowly, knife pointed straight ahead. Daniela stepped backwards until her back hit the wall. This was the end of her, but she brandished the pen in her hand and Sofia hesitated.

She lunged at Daniela, knocking the pen out of her hand. Daniela backed into a corner, wondering how she could have trusted this woman who was now going to kill her. But she wouldn't go down without a fight.

Sofia angled her head, drew closer, and swung the knife close to Daniela's throat. "Cameras in the room," she said. "He's watching. Can't hear us. Act as if you're scared."

Daniela gasped. Had she heard correctly? Had Santiago put hidden cameras in this room? "You're working with him, aren't you? That's why you know."

"I can explain," she said with gritted teeth. "Now act like you're scared and let's get out of this room. Then we'll talk."

Daniela played along, her eyes widening as Sofia held the knife at her back and pushed her into the foyer. She locked the building and breathed in the fresh air. Sofia put the knife into her bag. The midday warmth made her cheeks redden and her hands sweat. "What is going on?" She grabbed her bag with her mobile phone inside.

Sofia ushered her towards her parked car. "Get in."

Daniela sat in the passenger seat and looked Sofia squarely in the face. "What are you doing?"

"Before I explain everything, you need to understand I had no choice. He forced me, threatening to kill my family, my daughter, and then me. Like I said, I had no choice. He was watching my every move and I couldn't risk saying anything to you. I had to pretend everything was okay. I am so sorry. I never wanted this. None of it."

Was she on the level, Daniela wondered? How could she trust her after what had just happened? "You expect me to believe you when you let everything happen? Eva's kidnapping, Rafael's beating, and so much more."

"As I said, he was watching me everywhere. He has surveillance in my home, this place, and even in the bathroom here. I expect you to be sceptical, but let me explain." Daniela nodded. "Okay. I met Diego —"

"Wait, what? Diego? But he's your cousin, not my brother."

"No, he's someone I met when I was at the school on my own one night. He came into the building, pretending he had a daughter who wanted to do classes. Then he changed course and explained that he had a vendetta against you and your family, and that if I didn't help him with his plan, he would kill my family and me. I didn't believe him of course, until he showed me a video on his phone of my mother tied to a chair. He put a pillow over her face. Then the video stopped. I froze, wondering if he had killed my mother, but then he showed me another video untying her and letting her go. He said she would remain free if I did exactly as he said. That's when I started helping him. I was involved with everything right from the start; the fire, Eva's kidnapping, hurting Rafael, framing Fernando, and giving him my key to the building. I am so sorry."

Daniela had an epiphany. "If Diego isn't your cousin, then he has to be..."

"Who?"

"My brother." She took a calming breath. "I understand now why Rafael couldn't find Santiago."

Sofia stared straight ahead. "He changed his name so he could hide his real identity, but I didn't know anything about his history until you explained it to me. I suspected Diego might have been your brother, but I wasn't sure." She started the car.

"You need to tell me where he is," Daniela insisted. "What he's planning next."

"I will do better than that. I will take you to him. He's going to text me any minute now. He has no idea I'm on the other side now."

Daniela felt numb. "Why didn't you warn me about all this? Or give me a sign that you were being threatened? Even going to the police. You should have found a way."

Sofia swallowed, tears running down her cheeks. Wiping them away, she turned to her. "I tried going to the police just after you got that text message in the café, about Rafael. That's why I left early. I had to stop him from hurting you when I knew you loved Rafael."

"What happened that night?"

"I was right in front of the police station, determined to tell them the truth, when Diego ... Santiago stopped me. He dragged me to his car, kicking and screaming, and he drove me to my mother's house. When he stopped his car in front, I screamed and scratched his face, thinking he would hurt my mum, and begged him to leave her alone and swore that I wouldn't say anything. But he wouldn't listen, even when I explained how I wanted to protect my family. He held me at gunpoint as he pushed me in front of my mother's house and rang the doorbell. The street was quiet and all the houses were dark, so I assumed everyone was asleep. Before my mother could take a good look at Diego, he lunged at her and beat her to a pulp. I tried stopping him, but he punched me so hard, I was knocked out. Later, I woke up to find my mother lying on the living room floor, unconscious, with her face bloodied and bruised, and her arm broken. I sat there, frozen, before I called the ambulance and waited when I got a message on my phone from Diego saying, 'Next time you try to turn me in, she won't be so lucky.'"

Daniela's spine chilled as she stared fixedly at Sofia gripping the steering wheel. "That's why you had those few days off, because of that night, and what happened to your mother." Sofia nodded. "I am so sorry for what you went through, Sofia. How's your mother doing?"

"She's healing." Staring at the road ahead, she said, "I told you everything because I figure it will be our chance to kill him tonight. As I said, he thinks I'm still on his side, but I had to arrange protection tonight for my family. He doesn't know that my family's being guarded by an ex-military security guard. I've had enough of this, Daniela. Now that he wants to kill you all, that's where I draw the line. He doesn't know I can be just as ruthless to save my family, and he doesn't know that you know the whole story."

"What's your plan?"

"We need to sit tight until I hear from him." She looked at Daniela. "He's going to send you something. Where's your phone?" Daniela reached for it inside her bag. "But please, know that we're going to save them. He won't do anything until you get there."

"Save who? What are you talking about?" The silence unnerved Daniela. She felt like she couldn't breathe as she waited for the next phase of Santiago's game. Maybe this was a different kind of game. A game of where she would meet her doom, and may have to sacrifice herself to save her own family.

Resting her head back against the seat, she closed her eyes and willed this nightmare to be over. Why was Santiago punishing her? It wasn't like she had abandoned him. Hell, she hadn't even been born when her parents sent him away.

Her phone pinged, and holding it firmly in her hand, she stared at the horrifying display. She watched a video of her mother, gagged and blindfolded, hands bound to a chair behind her back. Her lip was split and her face was bruised. The video then showed Eva, who looked untouched, but was also gagged, blindfolded, and bound to a chair. Next to them, a fire smouldered over a piece of foil on a steel tray. A gasoline can and matches sat beside it. A text message pinged. "Race to save them. You have four hours." She stopped breathing and ignored the chill running down her back.

Sofia's eyes widened as she sped down the road. "We will save them, Daniela. I promise." She looked at her reassuringly, then faced ahead.

Daniela held on to the dashboard as Sofia raced through Madrid, running red lights. "Where are we going?"

"Santiago gave me this address in the Basque Country. In Bilbao. It's about four hours away, but I plan to make it in less than that. We'll save them. It's okay."

"He knows you're taking me there?"

"Yes, he knows, and he thinks I'm taking you to your death."

Daniela resigned herself to the possibility that she would die over this, but if she could save her family, she was okay with that. "I have to save my family."

Sofia nodded. "The plan is for you to give yourself to him in exchange for letting your family go. I think he plans to kill all of you. I'm so sorry, but I also have a plan."

"And what is it?" She pressed herself against the seat as Sofia drove well over the speed limit, narrowly missing a car that braked suddenly.

"I can't tell you, but trust me."

Daniela tried to call Rafael, but saw her battery was drained. "Oh, Christ! Can I use your phone to ring Rafael?"

Sofia nodded. "It's in the back seat in my bag. It's fully charged."

Daniela reached behind her and found Sophia's phone, but when she saw it, she moaned. "Your battery's dead, too. Do you have a charger?"

"At home." She slammed her hand against the steering wheel. "That wouldn't matter anyway. The bastard's hacked into our phone accounts and drained the batteries. He's an expert with technology. That means he doesn't even trust me, and that's not good."

"We don't even have time to stop to use my landline at home."

"No time at all, but we'll get there soon. I promise."

Daniela had bile in her throat and wanted to throw up, but she had to hold on to hope.

Chapter 51

A RAGING FIRE

D aniela sighed at the road accident up ahead. They were in Bilbao, so close, but this accident wouldn't clear up soon. They had only about fifteen minutes left on their timeline. "Do you think we'll make it, Sofia?"

She shrugged. "If it clears up soon, but it doesn't look like it's moving at all. I'm sure we'll be fine." Her words sounded flat, unconvincing.

Daniela steeled herself. "I'm getting out and running the rest of the way."

Sofia scoffed. "Are you crazy? You won't make it in fifteen minutes. It's at least a twenty- or twenty-five-minute walk."

Daniela said, "Who says I'm walking? I am making a run for it and saving my family. That bastard doesn't get to win."

Sophia tapped the wheel as she stared straight ahead. "I'll come with you."

Daniela shook her head. "No, you'll just hold me back, and you can't leave your car here. I'll be fine on my own. My inner rage will kill this guy." She opened her door and turned to Sofia. "Thanks for helping. If I don't make it, can you at least notify the police and make sure my brother is caught and punished?"

Sofia frowned. "You'll be fine, and I am not going to your damn funeral, so stay positive. Go straight until the intersection, then turn right. It's at the end of that road. Just go now or you'll never make it."

Daniela slammed the passenger door and ran faster than she ever had. She weaved between cars to a footpath parallel to the road. Her feet skidded on rubble, stones, dirt, and bark as she pushed ahead. She ignored passersby walking past her, and people in cars who stared at her as if she was completely mad. But she had to make it in time, and refused to give up. Surely her brother was playing another game and would not kill anyone. At worst, he'd wait for her and try to finish them off together. But she had a small knife in the back of her jeans, and she planned to use it.

If she weren't running for her family's life, she would have appreciated the green sloping mountain terrain, the fresh breeze, the towering trees surrounding the roads, and the stone houses in the distance. The fresh smell of pine and bark gave her renewed hope. Maybe her brother just wanted to put her on edge. This couldn't be the end, as she had so much to live for. She had found love after believing she never would. Daniela resolved to fight with every inner resource she had. She wouldn't let him win.

Gasping, she reached the intersection and stopped in her tracks to catch her breath. Then she turned right and raced down the dirt track over uneven ground. She could not see the stone house. Her throat was dry, her back ached, her legs felt like jelly, and her whole body was sweating, but she didn't care. She'd rest once she got there.

At least ten minutes passed, but she still couldn't see the house. Where was this place? All she could see were trees, sloping paths, and debris. She estimated that she had at least five more minutes. If only her phone was working, she could have messaged Santiago that she was on the way.

She had to stop again, huffing. When she caught her breath and started running again, she saw two stone houses ahead, a smaller stone one near a bigger house. She assumed he would keep her family in the smaller house while he remained in the larger one. Hope filled her spirit. Not far to go now. Only one hundred metres. She would make it. Just in time.

Rafael clenched the safety pin in his hand as Santiago pointed a gun in his face while giving him the key to unlock the door. "Open it." He opened the door then Santiago pushed him inside a large, bare living room, with dusty and dirty vinyl flooring and a multitude of windows. In a corner of the room, he froze at the sight before him. Adriana and Eva sat bound and gagged on chairs with their heads drooping. They stared at him with wide eyes, and made muffled noises through the gag. He flinched at the sight of a red gasoline container sitting underneath a steel tray. On the tray were a box of matches and a large piece of foil. *An explosion! He wanted to burn this house down.* "Give me your phone." Rafael retrieved his phone from his back pocket and handed it to him. Santiago placed it into his own back pocket.

Santiago cleared his throat. "Grab that chair from the kitchen and put it here, next to your friends. In better circumstances, she would have been your mother-in-law, but this bitch deserves to die."

Rafael headed into the kitchen, picked up a chair, and carried it towards Adriana. He set it beside her, knowing he had to think of a way to disarm Santiago, or they would meet a fiery end. "You won't get away with this."

He grimaced. "I already have. We will wait for Daniela to arrive. She should be here any minute now." Pointing the gun in his face, he turned briefly to reach for a coil of rope situated on the other side of the room. He threw the rope in his direction. "Tie yourself up." Rafael winced at the weight of the rope thrown at his feet while Santiago used one hand to pour the unlidded gasoline into the small piece of foil. His body shook at how close he was to causing a fire that would easily get out of hand. Fixing his gaze back on Rafael, Santiago kept pointing the gun in his direction. "I said tie yourself up."

"Why don't you do it? After you beat me, you weakened my hand. I can't do it."

Santiago sighed and stomped towards him, placing the barrel of the gun within inches of his face. "I don't care about your stupid hand. Now, tie yourself up or I will shoot you."

Rafael made out as if he was pulling at the rope when his right hand lifted. In one swift motion, he used his thumb and index finger that held the pin and rammed it into his eye. Santiago fell back and dropped the gun while his hand covered his eye, blood dripping around it. Quickly, Rafael's eyes scanned for the gun, which had fallen underneath Adriana's chair. With no time to grab it, he rushed over to Adriana and started untying the rope behind her hands. Santiago got up, raced towards him and punched him on the side of his cheek. Falling back, Rafael hit his head against the floor and the room spun around him. From the corner of his eye, he saw Santiago pick up the box of matches and flick one of the sticks against it. Flames licked to life. As he picked up the gasoline again, Rafael dashed towards him, accidentally spilling more gasoline onto the tin foil. He gasped and pushed Santiago to the ground, knocking him senseless with three punches to the face. Meanwhile, the fire raged, and the crackling sound increased his heart rate. "We have to get out of here."

For good measure, he swung two more punches into Santiago's face, then resumed freeing Adriana. She rubbed her hands then untied the cloth gag. He did the same for Eva. "No, this one's tight." Staring at Santiago, he breathed a sigh of relief, noticing he was unconscious.

Adriana pushed him aside. "Let me do it. I am good with knots." He looked for a blanket or a towel to put out the fire but couldn't see anything. Then again, why did he want to save this crazy man who had tried to kill them all? This crazy guy had beat him senseless, hurt Eva, threatened the love of his life, and had burned down her school. The rage inside him roared like the fire burning in the living room.

He removed the cloth gag from Eva when the last of the knot was undone and she was free. Scurrying to Santiago, he moved his hand underneath him, and reached for his phone. He pushed Adriana and Eva to the exit. "Let's go." The fire spread beyond the tray, and they coughed in the billowing smoke and fiery fumes. It was quickly spreading to the chairs and floor. Rafael and the others scurried to the exit and ran across a yard into the larger house. "Here, take my phone and call for help. I have to see if Daniela's here. Santiago said he was waiting for her to arrive, so she must be on her way."

Adriana wrapped her arms around him. "Thank you for saving us."

Eva moved to his side and touched him gently on the shoulder. "Thanks, Rafael. Go find Daniela. At least she is safe now."

Rafael heard a fiery explosion and jolted at the sound of screams. He ran to the front of the stone house to find Daniela lying on the ground, crying and screaming in pain. He ran towards her. "Daniela! Daniela."

Chapter 52

A CHALLENGE

Daniela breathed a sigh of relief when she had reached the grounds, and briefly closed her eyes to take a breath. She would save them.

But when a sudden, terrifying boom reverberated in her ears, and orange flames and black smoke flew out of the smaller stone house, she fell to her knees and screamed, "Noooo! Mum, Eva ... nooo ..." Daniela put her hands over her ears. The world spun around her. The weight in her chest and limbs made her droop as her vision blurred. Then she saw only black.

Daniela turned and rose at the sound of a familiar voice calling her name, her face wet with tears. The idea that her family was dead broke her heart, but seeing Rafael gave her hope. Had he saved them?

Rafael enclosed her in his arms and stroked the back of her head. "They're alive, Dani. They're alive. I got them out just in time."

Daniela caught her breath and sighed with relief. Tears of joy replaced the tears of sadness as her heart opened up again. "You saved them?"

Rafael nodded. "He was waiting for you, about to set the place on fire as soon as you got there. I think he's dead. We fought and I knocked him out. He was unconscious when the fire spread throughout that smaller house. He couldn't have survived that explosion."

Daniela caressed his face. "Oh, Rafael. Thank you. You have bruises. Are you okay?" He nodded. "He hurt us and my family for far too long. Where are they?"

"In the main house, but wait." He pressed his lips firmly on hers and kissed her with deep-seated, ravenous hunger. Daniela tantalised his tongue as she bit his lip and deepened the kiss. "I love you so much, Dani," he said. "I thought I had lost you. I never want to be separated from you again."

Daniela's heart warmed. "I love you too, Raf. More than I can express."

Someone cleared their throat behind them. "Well, isn't that touching? Love is all around. Hello, family," said Santiago.

Daniela slowly turned around, noticing Rafael's pallor as he held on to the small of her back. She stared down the barrel of a gun, then at Santiago's face. There was a bloody scar down the side of his eye, the bottom of it caked with dried blood. and partially closed. His hands had been slightly singed from the fire. She wondered if Rafael had done that to him. "Diego! Or should I call you Santiago?"

"Move. To the main house. I guess I'll need to kill you inside for more privacy. Where are the others, Rafael?"

"They've left. Probably in San Sebastian by now. But you failed, didn't you, creep?"

Santiago's eyes were dark pools of nothing. No emotion, just hardness. "I'll be the winner in the end, though, won't I?"

Daniela had to stall him until she could come up with a plan. She couldn't die without a fight. "Wait, Santiago. Before you kill us, I need to understand why you're doing this. What the hell did I ever do to you?"

He chuckled. "You had the life I wanted. What made you more worthy than me? Why didn't they give up you or Eva? I was their son, and they threw me away like a piece of garbage. I no longer had control over my life. But our dear father paid for turning me away, and your mother deserves the same fate. She might not die today, but I'll get her soon. Even your darling sister, Eva. She doesn't deserve to live, either. It was because of her that they gave me away. Before that bitch was born, I had all the attention. If she hadn't come, I would still be living with our parents. I had their love, but then Eva ruined everything. And you got to have what I always wanted."

Daniela pushed down her rage. "You tried to smother her with a pillow. What the hell did you expect? Roses? A reward? How could they trust you after that?"

Santiago scoffed. "I was their first, and they should have loved their son no matter what. I could have changed, but no, they never tried to talk to me about it. To understand why I did what I did. They judged and rejected me at eight. No one wanted me. Do you even know what that does to a child?"

Rafael intervened. "I take it you set up Daniela's father with the embezzlement charge, but he was innocent, wasn't he?"

Santiago nodded. "Pure genius if you ask me. That money went into my account, and I was able to fund my work activities." He glared at Daniela. "I forced him to leave his family. I told him that if he didn't leave you guys, that I would kill you all. He didn't want to leave you. The bastard loved you, but why should he live a good life when I didn't? When I was left behind."

Daniela felt her legs go weak beneath her. Her father had loved his family. He hadn't abandoned them of his own free will. "Why did you kill him when he did what you asked? He didn't deserve that, Santiago."

He leered again. "I was sick of his misery. He hadn't been punished enough for what he did to me. I had to kill him. The hate and the fury were too deep, and that was the only way to alleviate them."

Rafael shook his head as they stood close to the front door of the house. "And you even killed two people in foster care as well as Daniela's father. Anyone else?"

"I almost killed Teresa, my ex-wife, but she was a waste of my energy and time. I wanted her to live in fear, and I accomplished that. I know where she is. Living with her sister. Maybe I'll pay her a visit and kill her this time. Just for the control I can have over whether people get to live or die. It's a fun game when I get to move the pieces."

Rafael's spine chilled as he learned that Diego, or Santiago, was also Teresa's ex-husband. "So you've used different names. Javier, Diego. Do you even know who you are?"

He pushed them both inside the living room and prodded them over to the couch. Rafael held on to Daniela's hand as Santiago pushed them hard against it. "I know exactly who I am, Rafael. I am the master of my world. Whether I am Javier, Diego, or Santiago, I get to choose the life I want to live, and be who I want to be. No one tells me what to do or who to be anymore. I have that right."

Rafael snickered. "What about your daughter? Don't you care that she'll be without a parent?"

"I plan to get her back. I will teach her to be strong and have control. She will not be piss-weak and let people walk over her. I will teach her all the right things." He smirked.

"How did you kill my father?" Daniela demanded. "The autopsy showed he had a heart attack, but my father never had any heart issues."

He chuckled. "I used a combination of drugs that brought on heart failure. We shared a last drink together, then he went to bed and died.

I left a crossword puzzle by his side as my signature move. Brilliant, don't you think?"

Daniela wanted to kill him with her bare hands. "You psychopath. You don't deserve to breathe, and I hope that Karma gets you in the end."

He pointed the gun at Rafael. "I don't care what you think, sister." He grimaced. "I think I'll kill your friend first, so you can suffer longer. Then I'll kill you, Dani, my sister. A shame really. We could have got to know each other, and I could have pretended I liked your dance school. It was fun being Diego for a while. I got to know you. I even paid that motorcyclist to pretend to try to run you over, to win your trust. But I decided you weren't worth living the good life. One where you had family and I didn't."

"Please kill me first," Daniela pleaded. "Don't kill Rafael. Let him go. He has nothing to do with this. Please, Santiago. I beg of you. He won't tell anyone anything."

Santiago licked his lips and laughed, flailing the gun in their direction as he stood over them. "Oh, it turns me on how you are terrified right now. But I am the master, not you, not him."

Daniela saw Eva coming up behind him, carrying a lamp in both hands. She wound up and swung hard, smashing the lamp against Santiago's head. He fell and the gun fired. Eva screamed and fell, moaning in pain.

Rafael leaped onto Santiago. The gun flew out of his hand. Daniela rushed ahead and picked it up, pointing it at Santiago. She looked at her sister. Blood seeping through her pants, she gasped and closed her eyes as Daniela touched her calf.

Rafael took off his shirt and wrapped it around Eva's leg, tying it tightly while Daniela kept the gun pointed at Santiago. She had no idea how to use it, but Santiago did not know that. She feigned control of the gun until Rafael found rope on a kitchen counter, and tied him to the chair with his hands bound behind his back.

Daniela put the gun down on the bench. "You and your stupid games and puzzles. And you had the nerve to set my school on fire." He smirked until she punched him in the face, injuring her hand. Oh, but the pain was so worth it.

The sounds of sirens in the distance gave her hope that he would now be punished. Her mother raced towards Daniela and embraced her. "Oh, Mum. I am so glad you're okay. So glad."

"I am so sorry for all this, Daniela. Please forgive me."

"Sssh. I love you," was all Daniela said.

Santiago was going to prison for a long time.

Chapter 53

EPILOGUE

THREE MONTHS LATER

D aniela sat at the dinner table inside her home, smiling at her loved ones. Rafael bit into a chicken wing. Blanca sipped a glass of wine and laughed at a joke that Fernando made. Kim whispered something to Eva. Her mother bit into a carrot, and Carlos was in deep conversation with Sofia.

Rafael raised his glass of beer. "Why don't we toast to a life free of Santiago. At least we know the case against him is solid. He'll be going to prison for the rest of his life."

"Hear, hear," said Carlos.

Sofia cleared her throat. "I want to apologise to everyone here. If Diego hadn't beat up my mother so badly and threatened to kill my family, I would never have helped him. Please know that."

Blanca touched her gently on the shoulder. "It's okay. We understand. We all would have done the same thing to save our families."

Sofia smiled. "Thanks, Blanca."

Daniela remembered what Sofia had said in the car. "What was your plan while we were driving to Bilbao?"

Sofia drew back. "I was going to sacrifice myself for your family. I planned to provoke him and fight him to the end, even if it killed me."

Daniela clenched her hands. "Stupid plan, Sofia. I'm glad I got there before you did with the police."

Blanca leaned forward. "I take it Diego did everything to you. Set your school on fire, the kidnapping, Rafael's attack, and the messages. Then he put a bug in your room at the school so he could watch Sofia take you hostage and know what you were doing. Is that everything?"

Daniela nodded. "Pretty much. He killed my father because of the abandonment, and he set him up for the embezzlement. That money Santiago stole from the company went into his own private account, and he made it look as if it was coming from my father's account." She took a breath. "Santiago forced him to leave us, too. He still loved us."

Her mother's eyes lit up. "At least, darling, we know that Abel didn't truly leave us. He did that to keep us safe. I will sleep better at night now. May he rest in peace."

"I am so glad this is over," agreed Eva. "And may Dad rest in peace." They all toasted Abel Lopez, and fell silent for a few minutes.

After cleaning up and a last cup of coffee in their living room, Fernando pulled Rafael aside. He took a deep breath as he gripped his bottle of beer. "I am glad that guy's out of our lives. I know what I did was wrong, Raf, but I never meant to hurt my wife."

Rafael nodded. "What do you mean?" His friend remained silent. "That note I found, what was that about? And I saw you arguing with someone on the phone, too."

Fernando bowed his head, averting his eyes. "I did something stupid, Raf. I had an affair with an old girlfriend, Sara, and when I tried to break it off, she wouldn't accept it. She kept ringing me and I had to be forceful on the phone, but it didn't help. One night we met up at our usual hotel. We were talking in the lobby of the hotel when this person acting all drunk bumped into me, then when I asked for another drink because my glass was empty, I noticed the glass gone. I think the guy might have been Santiago, getting my fingerprints and framing me for your assault. The police mentioned how your bloodied shirt had my prints over them."

Rafael frowned. "I am sorry for what he did to you, Nando, but how could you do that to Rosalia? I thought you loved her."

"We've been having problems and we were separated at the time. I know it's no excuse, but the affair with Sara didn't last long. As soon as I realised I wanted to make things right, I broke it off with her. Sara sent me that note about keeping it a secret, so I can understand how you thought the worst. She wanted to make a plan about how we could make it work. Crazy, I know, but I would never hurt you, Raf. And I want to make things right with Rosalia."

"I know, but the situation made me paranoid. Now, you need to set things right in your marriage. Sort it out."

Fernando nodded. "I will." He touched him on the shoulder. "I am out of here, Raf. Take time off work and get some rest."

The others began to leave one by one. Carlos patted Rafael on the back. "Thank you for saving Daniela and her family, Rafael. Enjoy your night with Daniela. Blanca's staying with me tonight."

"Thanks, man," said Rafael.

Daniela hugged her friends, Blanca, Kim, and Sofia. "Take care, guys." She then wrapped her arms around her mother and sister. "See you soon, and I'm glad you guys are okay."

Daniela's mum wrapped her arms around Rafael. "Thank you for saving us, Rafael. I am so glad you are in Daniela's life. We'll invite you over for dinner soon."

Rafael beamed. "I look forward to it."

As soon as the guests left, Rafael led Daniela to the couch and stroked her cheek. "I love you so much, Dani. You are my light and my joy, and when I thought I'd lost you, I had this deep pit in the centre of my stomach. I had never known such pain and anguish. You're my world, and I want to be with you for the rest of our lives." He kissed her lightly on the lips.

"I do too, and I love you so much, Raf. I want to show you just how much in the bedroom."

He laughed. "First, Dani, can I ask you something?"

She angled her head. "Of course. What is it?"

He rushed into the kitchen and brought out a purple, gift-wrapped box that was as large as a computer monitor. "A special gift for you. Open it."

Daniela wondered what such a huge gift could be. "What is it?"

"You'll have to see. Open it."

Untying the ribbon around the box, she pulled off the lid. Inside was a smaller box. She opened it to find another box, and inside was yet another. A few more boxes later, she was left with a box small enough to fit on her palm. When she opened that one, she gasped at the gold ring inside. It had an oval diamond between two rectangular diamonds and glistened in the light. "It's beautiful, Raf."

"You're beautiful." He took the ring out of the box and placed it on her left ring finger. "Daniela Lopez. Will you do me the honour of being my wife? I will love you for the rest of our days."

Daniela shed tears, her heart swelling tenfold. "Oh, Raf. Of course, I'll be your wife. I love you." She leaned forward and kissed him gently.

"I love you too." He gave her a cheeky grin. "Now show me how much you love me."

Daniela laughed. "With pleasure." She led him towards her bedroom, knowing that she had a partner for life through the good times and the bad.

Reviews are gold to authors and allow Lucy to keep writing. If you enjoyed this story, please consider rating and reviewing it here: https://books2read.com/u/3JZe1X

Stay tuned for Book 3 of the Women Of Strength Series.

In the meantime, if you haven't read Book 1 (*In Rio's Shadows*) of the Women Of Strength Series, about Blanca, here is the link: https://books2read.com/u/mq1qP8

ABOUT THE AUTHOR

Lucy Appadoo is a prolific reader and author of the Friends In Crisis Series. After a childhood spent reading and imagining escapist worlds, Lucy has put her imagination into stories. Her work as a rehabilitation counsellor, and
former work as a counsellor in private practice, have led to an interest in writing inspirational stories about authentic, driven women who manage adversity with strength and heart. She writes in the genres of romantic suspense/thrillers with significant life themes and contemporary romance.

Lucy's interests include researching crime stories and news to inspire her work, watching crime thrillers and suspenseful movies, travel, exercising, reading for entertainment or knowledge, meditation, and spending time with friends and family. She also appreciates her Italian background and culture, which has inspired her to write imaginative stories about her parents' childhoods, leading to The Italian Family Series novels.

Check out Lucy's website and sign up for a FREE romantic suspense novel here: www.lucyappadooauthor.com.au

ABOUT THE AUTHOR

ALSO BY LUCY APPADOO

Short Story Thrillers

Evening Interrupted: https://books2read.com/u/3yZDjZ

The Dreamcatcher: https://books2read.com/u/bzaLxn

Red Flags: https://books2read.com/u/bWZ9W1

Collection of Short Story Thrillers: https://books2read.com/u/bP5vwj

The Italian Family Series - Coming of Age Family Drama

A New Life: https://books2read.com/u/mqqwZm

The Beauty of Tears: https://books2read.com/u/bpqwk3

Dancing in the Rain: https://books2read.com/u/bOr7LA

A Life By Design: https://books2read.com/u/3J8ene

NON-FICTION

Grief & Loss

Moving Beyond Grief - How To Shift From Grief & Loss to Joy & Peace: https://books2read.com/u/mVNzDA

Stress Management & Anxiety

Holistic Spiritual and Mental Health - Building Resilience and Creativity by Conquering Anxiety and Managing Stress: https://books2read.com/u/47kG8A

Career Guidance

Your Holistic Career Path - Create Career Change, Satisfaction, and
Work/Life Balance: https://books2read.com/u/bzYDz4